LA LUCIA

La Lucia – A story of Riseholme in the Style of the Originals by E.F.Benson
Hugh Ashton

ISBN-13: 978-1-912605-72-9

ISBN-10: 1-91-260572-4

Published by j-views Publishing, 2020

www.HughAshtonBooks.com

www.j-views.biz

publish@j-views.biz

j-views Publishing, 26 Lombard Street, Lichfield, WS13 6DR, UK

CONTENTS

INTRODUCTION

This is the third Mapp and Lucia pastiche that I have produced – and it has taken me longer to write it than it took to write the other two, partly because it does in fact contain more words, and partly because of personal family matters.

There is another reason why this particular book took longer to produce – it was more difficult to write.

Writing a prequel is in many ways more tricky than writing a sequel. Characters are already defined in the originals, and though in a sequel it is possible to develop a character and add changes to the previously written personality, it is not as easy to write a character radically different to the original who will then magically metamorphise into something different when he or she makes his first appearance in the original. Briefly, characters in a prequel must be truer to the originals than in a sequel.

In the case of Lucia stories, writing about Riseholme is more difficult than writing about Tilling. The setting and characters are not as sharply drawn – after all, Riseholme and its inhabitants appear in the entirety of only one book (*Queen Lucia*) and almost in passing in two more (*Lucia in London* and *Mapp and Lucia*). By contrast, Tilling society has over three entire books devoted to it. There is therefore less ore available from which a writer may extract the gold, though the quality of the gold is equal to that which my be mined from Tilling.

However, the absence of Elizabeth Mapp-Flint (*née* Mapp) does deprive the writer of a rich lode of material. I found, however, that Mrs Jane Weston can be channelled relatively easily, and that her long rambling discourses were quite easy for me to write. Perhaps I was copying my maternal grandmother's style of conversation, which in many ways echoed that of Mrs Weston.

Writing light social comedies in the time of

a pandemic-induced recession might seem to some to be inappropriate, or even somewhat heartless. However, it appears that the first two offerings filled a need for more Tilling stories than E.F.Benson originally produced, and according to most readers who gave their opinion, I hit several nails on the head in terms of setting, characterisation, and plotting. I am delighted to have given so much pleasure to so many through these books.

Very special thanks to my friend Victoria Yardley, who took the trouble to read through what I had innocently assumed was a print-ready manuscript and found more tarsome infelicities and outright errors than I ever would have imagined to exist. All remaining misteaks are mine.

I trust that this slice of Riseholme life can do the same in its bringing to life of several events that were mentioned in the original books, but were never described in the detail that they deserve.

So, I bid you *au reservoir*, until the next time.

Hugh Ashton
Lichfield, 2020

LA LUCIA

A STORY OF RISEHOLME IN THE STYLE
OF THE ORIGINALS BY E.F.BENSON

HUGH ASHTON

J-VIEWS PUBLISHING, LICHFIELD, UK

PROLOGUE

Mrs Emmeline Lucas had been heard on more than one occasion to complain that the number of hours in the day was insufficient.

"Another two or three," she remarked, "would allow me to do more than the little I achieve now."

To which, her husband's customary reply was, "But *Lucia mia*, you do so much already, it is hard to know what else might be accomplished."

The use of the Italian phrase to address her was a consequence of the couple comprising the Lucas family of Riseholme letting it be known that they conversed with each other in Italian on a regular basis. For *la Lucia*, meaning 'the wife of Lucas', or simply Lucia, as she had become known to the quaint little village where they lived, was a true adept of all that pertains to culture, be it literature, music, painting, or drama. Italian, being the language of the arts, must perforce be her language of choice, though she reconciled her use of humdrum everyday English with the thought that it was the language of the divine Bard of Avon.

Accordingly, Lucia's husband, though he pleaded before the Bar as Philip Lucas, was Italianised in Riseholme as Pepino, and he answered readily enough, albeit in English, when so addressed. Though he cheerfully acknowledged the superiority of his wife with regard to the production of music and watercolour painting, he himself was no stranger to the arts, with prose poems, typically composed on abstract and lofty subjects, forming his contribution for posterity.

Their dwelling, The Hurst, consisted of three cottages, joined together and extended in a resolutely Elizabethan style and overlooking the village green. Those parts of the building which were reportedly of the time of Good Queen Bess were made even more so redolent of that age, and those proclaiming themselves as being of a later vintage were replaced by more modern substitutes, cunningly disguised to appear as old, if not older, than the genuine articles.

Inside, though modern conveniences such as electric light and modern forms of heating existed, the overall impression of the house was that the creator of *Hamlet* could have walked into the dwelling and felt himself at home. Indeed, the guest bedrooms were named after the plays and the characters that he had brought to life on the stage.

Not only the house, but the garden also showed the influence of Shakespeare on the lives of Lucia and Pepino – a whole border was devoted to those flowers listed by Perdita in *The Winter's Tale*, and other literary references were scattered throughout the flowers, engraved on stone tablets.

When Lucia was not busy with practising the works of noble Beethoven or delicious Mozart on her grand piano, or studying the works of the literary masters in English or Italian (the latter with the aid of a crib and a dictionary), she was often to be found in the garden, enjoying her flowers, and planning entertainments, such as garden-parties, musical evenings, or tableaux and charades, for the amusement of her neighbours.

Though some might consider Riseholme to be a sleepy backwater, those who lived there were constantly kept on the boil with the excitement generated by the actions of the other inhabitants, and the activity, not to mention the gossip, that resulted from these, filled their days.

Lucia who by her natural talents, with the aid of her determined efforts, had made herself acknowledged as the leader of social activity in Riseholme, was responsible for most of these crazes, though she sometimes faced a little competition from others, chiefly Daisy Quantock, who also resided on the green, overlooking the village ducking pond (sometimes referred to by the vulgar as merely "the duckpond") and the site of the village stocks, which had been rescued and were scheduled for presentation to the village by Lucia and Pepino. Despite the occasional minor rebellions by Daisy, sometimes encouraged by her husband Robert, it was generally admitted that the crown of Tilling rested firmly on Lucia's head, and that it would take little short of a full-blooded Bolshevik revolution to dislodge it.

ONE

One spring day, Lucia was digging in her garden with a view to enriching the soil around her roses. She had begun this exercise somewhat light-heartedly, but soon found herself beginning to tire of the stooping and bending involved.

The arrival of her neighbour and closest friend in Riseholme, Georgie Pillson, gave her a welcome excuse to straighten her back, and she did so with a sigh of relief.

"*Georgino mio*," she exclaimed. "Any news?" The first part of this little speech was an allusion to the notion that the Lucases included Georgie Pillson as an integral part of their Italian circle. The second part was a common greeting in Riseholme. By 'news', the inhabitants of this quaint village did not signify the everyday business of the nation. Of infinitely more importance than recent speeches by the Prime Minister were matters such as whether Daisy Quantock had or had not taken up some new form of diet, or a report on the details of old Mrs Antrobus's new ear-trumpet. Such matters were of great interest to Riseholme and could provide topics of conversation for several days on end.

Since their separate arrivals in Riseholme some years earlier, Lucia and Pepino having made their move some two months after Georgie's settling in the village, the Lucases and Georgie Pillson had become great friends, finding common areas of enjoyment in music, painting (both Lucia and Georgie painted pretty little watercolours) and other artistic endeavours; not to mention an intense interest in the doings of other Riseholmites. It had been only a matter of days before the 'Mr Pillsons' and 'Mrs Lucases' had become 'Georgies' and 'Lucias'. Indeed, it was hard to think of Georgie as 'Mr Pillson'. His real age, although a guarded secret, was by common consent estimated to be higher than the publicly proclaimed value, but his perpetual air of youth (aided, whispered a few, by the application of certain liquids to the hair), had earned him the right to be 'Georgied' by all.

"Not much of interest," he said with a negligent air which would fool nobody, least of all Lucia, regarding the importance of what he was about to say. "But I thought you might like to see this." He motioned towards the marketing basket that he was carrying. "Come and sit with me on this bench and I will show you."

Lucia, intrigued by her courtier's air of mystery, sat on the garden bench as Georgie carefully removed a cloth from the basket, and proceeded to unfold it, revealing a few fragments of shining glass.

"There!" he said, triumphantly. "Don't you think they are splendid?"

Lucia cocked her head on one side, and regarded the pieces quizzically. "I am not sure what I am supposed to say," she answered at length. "Am I to commiserate with you on Foljambe's clumsiness?" Foljambe was the improbable name of Georgie's peerless parlour-maid, who was as likely to break one of his possessions as she was to take wing and fly from the attic window over the village green.

"No, no," he said impatiently. "See here," pointing to a curiously shaped piece of glass which glistened in the sun with a coat of many colours. "And here," he added, pulling a thick book from the bottom of the basket. Lucia read the title on the spine, *The Romans in Britain*, by Professor Arbuthnot.

Georgie had marked a place in the book with a slip of paper, and opened it there to reveal a drawing of a beautifully shaped glass vessel with a handle. "Now see here. This part of the handle in the picture exactly matches this piece of glass, does it not?"

Lucia scrutinised the page and the glass shard. "I believe you may be correct," she admitted at length.

"So this is Roman glass," Georgie finished triumphantly. "And who knows what else might be there?"

"Where is 'there'?" asked Lucia, her curiosity now fully awakened.

"Long Meadow, just by the river. I think it was just before you and Pepino came to Riseholme that the Professor Arbuthnot who wrote this book – he's from the British Museum – came to stay at the Ambermere Arms and told us that there had been a Roman villa built there over one and a half thousand years ago. And now they are ploughing up the field."

Lucia's eyes shone with excitement. "And how

did you come to find this lovely object?" she asked him. In her eyes, the glass in Georgie's hand had now moved from being a fragment of a dish broken by Foljambe to being an exciting archaeological find.

"I saw they were ploughing the field, and I remembered what Professor Arbuthnot had said, so I decided to see if anything had turned up. I saw something shining, and this is what I found. It was quite a tarsome business, and I got my hands and boots muddy, and the bottom of my trousers may never be quite the same again, but I think it was worth it, don't you?"

"Just imagine, Georgie," Lucia said, the gabbling tone with which Georgie had recently become familiar making its way into her voice. "Just imagine, if we were to discover some real Roman treasure. How wonderful that would be, to find an amphitheatre or a temple, and all those marvellous things that the Romans brought with them to these islands."

"I don't think the Professor said anything about a temple or an amphitheatre," said Georgie, hesitantly. "And in any case, an amphitheatre would be a rather horrid thing to find, when you think of all the animals and gladiators and things that might have died there. But a complete villa would be exciting enough."

"Indeed it would," Lucia agreed. "We should do this properly, though. Trowels and brushes and sieves are what these people use, I believe. And we shouldn't be greedy, should we, Georgie? Everyone should have a chance to collect these beautiful things and make discoveries." She paused, seemingly lost in thought. "I know, I shall invite everyone to a little party tomorrow night, and you can tell them about your discoveries, and I can give a little impromptu talk on Roman Britain to prepare us all, and then we can all start our researches the next day."

Georgie shuddered. "I'm sure I shan't be able to talk about my discoveries," he said. "I'm no good at all about that sort of thing, and I'm sure they won't want to listen to me as well as to you. Much better for only you to talk. But if anyone wants to ask me any questions about what I found, of course I will be happy to answer them."

"Very well, then. Whom should we invite?"

"Daisy and Robert Quantock, to start," Georgie answered, counting on his fingers. "And Mrs Weston, that's three. "Colonel Boucher, four. Mrs Antrobus, though she won't be able to hear very well, and her two daughters, that's seven. The Vicar and Mrs Rumbold, nine. And you and Pepino and me, that's eleven."

"Lady Ambermere?" suggested Lucia.

"I don't think that would be a very good idea," Georgie told her. "I can't really imagine her digging in a field, even if it was to discover Roman remains. "And she would want to bring that nasty horrid Pug of hers with her, and it would fight with the Colonel's bulldogs."

"Very well, then," said Lucia. "Are you quite sure you don't want to speak?"

"Quite sure," said Georgie, firmly.

"May I ask you to invite everyone to The Hurst tomorrow at eight o'clock? You might add that maybe we could enjoy a little music after the talk?"

"It sounds delightful," said Georgie. "But we haven't practiced that new Mozart yet."

"Never mind," said Lucia without pausing. "I will play the first movement of the 'Moonlight Sonata' – the perfect music to set the mood." She paused. "Perhaps you could lend me your book there. Just to remind me of some of the details. Dates and so on, and the wonderful names that the Romans had for our towns."

"Of course," said Georgie, handing the book to her.,

"And no more excavations without me," Lucia commanded.

"Of course not," agreed her devoted subject.

TWO

For that day and the next, nothing was to be seen or heard of Lucia, other than that on the following morning a few bars of something that sounded suspiciously like the new Mozart crept out of the windows of The Hurst, being played slowly with the soft pedal of the piano firmly depressed.

For his part, Georgie went around the village, starting with his next-door neighbour, Daisy Quantock.

"Well, that does sound interesting," she said, after she had heard what Georgie had to say, and extended Lucia's invitation to her. "Not that it wouldn't be hard work bending and digging in that field, but I dare say that there might be something worth finding there. According to Madame Evantis, the stars tell me I will discover something valuable in the next few days."

It should be explained here that Daisy Quantock was a great taker-up (and putter-down) of beliefs and crazes. Currently, astrology was her great passion, and she received weekly forecasts from a Madame Evantis, whose name she had discovered in a magazine devoted to such matters which had been left behind in a railway carriage by an earlier traveller.

She had been enthusiastically assailing all her friends with demands for precise details of the place and exact time of their birth, in an attempt to gain greater understanding of their characters and their futures. However, no one seemed able to provide these precise details, and Daisy was forced to rely merely on the day that her friends were born. According to Madame, this was not sufficient to provide her clients with accurate forecasts. However, her prophecy that he would find true love and marry within the year had sent Georgie into a state of nervous near-collapse, despite his protestations to Lucia (who refused to have anything to do with the whole business) that he could not find it in himself to believe in such nonsense.

Robert Quantock, Daisy's husband, was less than enthusiastic about his wife's 'stunt', and had no time for what the stars and planets might have to say about his future or his financial investments, and even less time, if possible, for the prospect of a Roman villa. "Don't know how you can be so sure that they are Roman," was his verdict after examining Georgie's prized bits of glass. "Could be ten years old, might be fifteen hundred. I'll come along to hear Lucia speak, if that's what she wants, but don't expect me to get my hands, and probably the rest of me, dirty for the sake of a few pieces of old rubbish."

Georgie had a little more luck with Colonel Boucher. "Ha! Fascinating, what?" he exclaimed after taking a brief look at the glass that Georgie showed him and listening to the explanation of how and where it had been found. "Yes, I remember the professor johnny from London telling us about the Roman villa. Thought it was all safely gone and buried, but it seems that it's coming to the surface again. Buried treasure, eh? Who knows? You can tell Mrs Lucas that I look forward to her evening tomorrow."

Cheered by this reception, Georgie prepared to visit old Mrs Antrobus, who lived with her two daughters, known to all as Piggy and Goosie. Informing Mrs Antrobus of any recent happenings was hard work, partly on account of her deafness, which seemed to get worse every year, but also on account of Piggy and Goosie who appeared to have discovered the secret of eternal youth (at least in their own minds), and even long after their age would seem to have forbidden – or at the very least, strictly frowned upon – such antics, skipped and gambolled around the village like a pair of schoolgirls.

Piggy especially had noted Georgie down as an eligible bachelor – eligible, that is, as a possible husband for herself, and Georgie had to take good care never to find himself close to her, in order to avoid the little dabs and pecks which she seemed determined to bestow on him, all the while giggling girlishly.

Accordingly, when he was ushered into the sitting-room, Georgie took care to seat himself next to Mrs Antrobus on the narrow sofa in such a way that there was no way for Piggy or Goosie, let alone both of them, to sit beside him. There was the additional advantage of being able to speak directly into Mrs Antrobus's ear-trumpet, which meant that he did not need to repeat things more than two or three times before their meaning became apparent to her.

"Any news?" was her greeting to him as he settled himself.

"I found these," he shouted into her trumpet, revealing the pieces of glass that he had discovered in the field.

"Oh dear," said Mrs Antrobus, examining the fragments curiously. "I am sorry that you broke it. Was it very expensive?"

"No, it was in the field, in Long Meadow," Georgie said.

"What on earth were you doing with it in the field?" asked Mrs Antrobus. "I swear, I don't understand you young people today."

Georgie was torn between frustration at being unable to explain his finds to Mrs Antrobus, and pleasure at being included in the group of 'young people', though he had to admit to himself that Mrs Antrobus's view of what constituted 'young' would have been unfairly influenced by Piggy and Goosie. He tried another tactic.

"Lucia has invited you to her house at eight o'clock tomorrow evening," he said.

"What for?"

"She wants to tell us all about Roman villas," Georgie said, loudly and distinctly.

"Roaming in villages?" asked Mrs Antrobus, puzzled.

"No, mamma," said Piggy, bouncing up and down on her chair in excitement, and repeating "Roman villas" very loudly and distinctly.

"Oh yes, I remember that professor from the Museum coming and telling us all about the one in Long Meadow." She stopped, having assembled the pieces of the puzzle in her mind. "Oh, so these are pieces of Roman glass, are they, Mr Georgie? How exciting."

"And Lucia wants to talk about Roman villas tomorrow, mamma," said Goosie. "Oh do let's go." Like her sister, she bounced up and down with excitement.

"Oh yes," chorused Piggy, bouncing in unison with her sister.

"Oh, very well then," said Mrs Antrobus. "Eight o'clock, you say? How long do you think she will be speaking for?"

"No more than an hour, I would think," Georgie answered her, though he was actually unsure of what sort of length Lucia's 'impromptu' talk would be, given the effort she would almost certainly put into its preparation. "So we can expect to see all three of you?" he said.

Having received a positive answer, he moved on to the Vicarage, where Mrs Rumbold informed him that her husband was currently engaged on some errand of mercy, but pledged that both he and she would be present at Lucia's talk, though she could not speak for either of them being available to carry out any of the actual excavations.

Encouraged by this response, Georgie moved to his last port of call, namely Mrs Weston, who was easily the best observer and recounter of observations in Riseholme, despite the fact that she was confined to a bath-chair.

"Well, I really don't know," she said, after inspecting Georgie's pieces of glass and being invited to guess where he had found them. "I do declare that is just like the handle of a jug that Mr Weston used to have, which he inherited from his aunt, the one who used to live in Hastings and who married the man who invented a new kind of safety-valve to go on railway engines, and which he broke one afternoon after he came in from playing golf with the Vicar. I remember that he went round in eighty-three strokes, and the Vicar went round in eighty-two, but he said the Vicar had cheated by moving his ball out of a bunker when he thought no one was looking." She inspected

Georgie's treasure trove a little more closely. "I was just talking about this last week with Colonel Boucher when he was coming out of Rush's and he had ordered half a pound of currants because Rush said he had no raisins, and why he had no raisins I couldn't say if you begged me to tell you because he had some two weeks ago and Cook made a very nice pudding out of them. I couldn't eat it all, and Cook and Elizabeth said they were the best raisins they had ever eaten in a pudding. And the Colonel said he had played golf and lost by one stroke and that put me in mind of that day and it was also the day the German Emperor made a speech about something which annoyed the Prime Minister and that was the very same day that Mr Weston broke the jug." She paused for breath. "And how you ever got hold of that handle I don't know, because I remember giving it to Elizabeth to throw away. 'Wrap it up well,' I said to her, 'because someone might cut their hand on it and die of blood-poisoning like old Mr Marlowe who cut his thumb when he was raking the flowerbed in his front garden and he got blood-poisoning and died two— no, three weeks later, and then we'd get the blame.' So what she did with it, I couldn't tell you, but I haven't seen it from that day to this when you showed it to me just now and I really have no idea where you might have found it."

Georgie told her that he had discovered it in Long Meadow, and that he strongly suspected it of being substantially older than Mr Weston's jug of several years ago. Mrs Weston appeared suitably impressed, and naturally (for Mrs Weston had by far the best memory for detail of anyone in Riseholme) remembered the words of Professor Arbuthnot regarding the probability of a Roman villa there.

"I shall certainly come to hear what Lucia has to say about it all," she said to Georgie, "though I dare say she will have got it all out of books that anyone can read for themselves, but it might be interesting all the same. But if she's expecting me to dig for these things, I won't be doing it myself, but Henry Luton will push me there and dig for me, I dare say. Now the weather's getting warmer again and the evenings are getting longer, it will be good for us all to be getting out into the fresh air. And who knows what we might find?"

"Indeed," agreed Georgie, and made his way back to Lucia in some sort of triumph.

THREE

"**Y**ou *have* done well, Georgie," she told him when he told her of the responses to her invitation. "Pepino has very kindly agreed to give a brief introduction, which should not take more than twenty or thirty minutes, and my talk should not take more than an hour and a half. I shall start with the foundation of Rome, with the wolf and Romulus and Remus, and move through the period of the Republic, ending with Julius Caesar's invasion of Britannia, and then the later invasion by Claudius. Then I can really start to go into detail about how these wonderful Romans brought so many things here – heating, edible snails, mosaics, edible dormice – yes, Georgie, the Romans ate dormice. I can't imagine it, but they probably thought they were delicious. Of course, my explanation will all have to be very superficial, crammed into such a short space of time, and I can hardly do justice to the subject, but I should be able to cover the highlights. We will have a period for questions, perhaps an hour? And then some delicious Beethoven to send everyone home."

"It sounds delightful," said Georgie. "But I don't think that Piggy and Goosie will be able to sit still for that long. And Mrs Weston has said in the past that she hardly ever goes to bed after ten, and I think we should take her feelings into account."

"Yes, those are very good points," said Lucia who, truth be told, was more relieved than otherwise at the prospect of abbreviating her talk. "Perhaps for the sake of Piggy and Goosie, and poor Mrs Weston, we might make the evening a little shorter."

"I'm sure that will be better for them," Georgie agreed. "And Pepino won't need to make such a long introduction."

Pepino, who had entered the room during this conversation, concurred with this judgement. Although a seasoned courtroom advocate who could plead a case for several hours

without intermission, he was less than enthusiastic about the idea of introducing Lucia,
who after all needed no introduction, to their
neighbours, for half an hour on end.

"Now I will want you, Georgie, to take charge
of the guests and sit them in the right places.
Mrs Antrobus must sit at the front, of course,
and I will take care to speak in her direction as
often as I can. I suppose Piggy and Goosie must
sit near her. Mrs Weston must have a place
where Henry Luton has plenty of space for her
bath-chair. And the Vicar and Mrs Rumbold,
and Colonel Boucher... Did he say whether he
was going to bring his bulldogs, Georgie?"

"No, he didn't say."

"Let us hope that he will not, though I fear
that he will," said Lucia.

"And then Robert and Daisy Quantock," said
Georgie. "And me, of course."

"But you will take a seat on the platform, of
course, with Pepino and me," said Lucia.

"You are having a platform?" asked Georgie
incredulously.

"No, no, merely a figure of speech," said Lucia.
"I only meant that you should sit at the front
facing the audience. After all, you are the one
who discovered the first Roman remains."

"Well, it's most terribly kind of you to say

that, and to ask me to share this platform with you, but I really don't think I could manage it. People might expect me to speak, and that would be awful if I did, or they might wonder what I was doing sitting with you and Pepino if I wasn't speaking, and that would be awful, too."

"Very well, then," said Lucia, "if you really do feel that strongly about it."

"I do."

Pepino cleared his throat. "You know, Lucia mia, I don't believe you really need my introduction. These are our friends and neighbours, after all."

"Very well then," said his wife brightly. "We will have a much more simple and informal gathering. Simply old friends sitting and talking together about something that is sure to be of interest to everyone. Yes? Then that's settled."

Georgie was much relieved by this decision. The thought of standing up and making a speech, even to a few old friends, or even answering their questions in such an assembly, was one which filled him with terror, and caused him to shrink into himself.

"And you'll be joining Pepino and me this

evening for dinner before we start the talk, won't you?"

"Well," said Georgie, "I had ordered lamb chops..."

"Exactly what we will be eating," said Lucia brightly. "So that's settled."

As so often, Georgie felt himself to be in the grip of a powerful whirlwind which carried him over anything that resembled an obstacle without considering the consequences.

"And now," said Lucia, "do you have time for a little *Mozartino*? The arrangement of the 'Jupiter' for four hands has just arrived, and we could try reading it."

"Very well, but not for too long. After that I must go back and tell Foljambe and Cook that I won't be dining at home tonight, and then change for dinner," said Georgie. "Which part shall I take?"

"The bass, I think," said Lucia. "It needs a man's firm hand. Jupiter, you know, the king of the gods."

Georgie seated himself at the left of the stool, and took off several of his rings in order to give his fingers more flexibility. As he did so, he cast an eye over Lucia's part, and recognised it as the music he had heard earlier as he passed by The Hurst. "Why she has to pretend all the time, I don't know," he thought to himself, but told himself that it was simply pretty Fanny's way. He placed his hands on the keys, and waited for Lucia's count.

"*Uno, duo, tre*," she sang out, and they crashed their way through the first movement.

"I feel quite exhausted," Georgie told Lucia, bringing out a large burgundy silk handkerchief and fanning himself with it.

"Such powerful music from *divino Mozartino*," Lucia agreed. "Shall we try the next movement?"

"No, I must go and get ready for this evening. How exciting it is. What do you think we shall find, when we're all busy digging away?"

"Lots and lots of wonderful things," said Lucia. "Hypocausts, for example."

"I remember those," said Georgie. "Those are the pipes that carried hot air around the house to heat it, aren't they?"

"That's right, and if we find any evidence, that means that the owner of the villa must have been rather wealthy, and we might find all sorts of interesting things."

"Roman bibelots?"

"Yes, what a wonderful way of describing them. With your permission, I would like to use that in my talk later this evening."

"Of course you may, Lucia. But I really must be off. Foljambe hates being rushed and I really don't want to upset her."

"Very well. Lamb chops here at seven, remember. *Arrivederci.*"

FOUR

Georgie returned just before seven, clad in his dinner jacket with a mauve cummerbund. If anyone had taken the trouble to look, his socks, largely hidden by his patent leather shoes, were of the same hue, and a matching triangle of handkerchief protruded from his breast pocket.

The meal was eaten in near silence, at least as far as Georgie and Pepino were concerned. Lucia kept up a stream of chatter, the subject of which was mostly, but not always, connected with the wisdom she was preparing to unleash on the heads of the inhabitants of Riseholme.

At length, the meal was ended, and Lucia led the way into the drawing-room, where

Grosvenor, the parlour-maid, had previously arranged the chairs in a kind of semicircle around a high-backed chair, which was presumably to form the throne from which Lucia would address her subjects.

Robert and Daisy Quantock were the first to arrive, and Grosvenor greeted them each with a glass of sherry, received with avidity by Robert, who immediately drained his portion, whereupon it was refilled without delay.

Daisy, for her part, proclaimed to the bemused Pepino that for her to take such refreshment would be unwise at this time, given that Saturn was rising, and that Mercury was in Gemini, a statement that apparently she understood, even if she was the only member of the party who did.

Mrs Weston appeared next, her bath-chair pushed by Henry Luton, and she gladly accepted the proffered glass. "Thank you, Mr Lucas," she began. "I must say that this reminds me so much of the times when Mr Weston and I had friends to dinner. Mr Weston always used to order his sherry from Bristol, and he said that you could never go wrong with the wine merchants he used. The firm was called Sparrow's, and that's a strange name, isn't it, and I always remember it because my aunt had a maid who was called Jenny, and if you can believe it, she married a Mr Wren. So she was always Jenny-Wren to us, and we used to have a good laugh about it, I can tell you."

At this point, Colonel Boucher and his two bulldogs made their appearance, and Henry pushed the bath-chair, with Mrs Weston still talking, into the centre of the room, where a gap in the seats indicated its intended place.

The Reverend and Mrs Rumbold arrived, and accepted the offered refreshment before moving to the seats to which Pepino ushered them.

Mrs Antrobus and her two daughters arrived last, with Mrs Antrobus brandishing an enormous ear-trumpet to ensure that she would not miss a single word of Lucia's talk. Explaining that she needed both hands to manage this monstrosity, she refused the offered glass of sherry, leaving her two daughters to argue prettily, with many glances turned in Georgie's direction to ensure that he missed none of the discussion.

"I'm not sure that you should be drinking sherry, Goosie," Piggy told her sister. "You know how it always goes to your head."

Goosie giggled. "Fancy your saying that!" she exclaimed. "I remember the time when you drank just a few sips of cider and started singing 'Pop Goes the Weasel' so loudly that even mamma could hear you."

"Well, if you're going to say that, you silly Goosie, I could also mention the time when—"

She was interrupted by Lucia herself who drove them, as a dog drives sheep, to the two chairs which had been provided for them, one on either side of their mother, before taking the stage.

Pepino and Georgie, who had gratefully accepted the loss of their supporting roles, took their seats near the door.

Lucia opened by reminding her audience of the conquest of Britain by the Romans, and their subsequent occupation over several centuries.

"As you may imagine, many of the Romans settled in Britannia, as we were known then, just as we English have settled in India and in other parts of the globe, and built houses and villas where they could live in luxury unimaginable to the natives." (At this point Georgie recognised a sentence from the book which he had lent to Lucia) "And here in Riseholme we are extremely fortunate, as Professor Arbuthnot of no less an institution than the British Museum itself, has declared that under Long Meadow lie the remains of a Roman villa.

"Now Long Meadow has been put under the plough, and though we may regret the loss of this grazing land, where we have enjoyed the sight of sheep peacefully grazing, as the composer Johann Sebastian Bach reminded us in that great chorale of his, there is a silver lining to this cloud. Mr Pillson, who needs no introduction to anyone here, was walking there, and he came across these."

Here she removed the cover from a dish standing on a small table beside her with a dramatic flourish, and revealed the fragments of glass that Georgie had discovered. Since the members of the audience had all seen these previously, there were no gasps of surprise or wonder, much to the disappointment of Lucia, who had seemingly forgotten that Georgie had previously displayed them to the audience now before her. However, she pressed on, undaunted.

"These exquisite pieces of glasswork are very clearly those made and used by those wonderful Romans who lived here so long ago," she declared. "Possibly part of some sacrificial vessel – there may be a temple beside the villa. And I think I may safely conclude that there will be other magnificent things to be found – perhaps some golden coins with the heads of some of those emperors, or more sacrificial vessels, or even some of those beautiful Roman jewels that the women of that time wore." Here Lucia launched into a long description of life in Roman times, which Georgie recognised from his reading of the book. As she expounded, he was torn between admiration for her cleverness in absorbing all this knowledge so quickly, and a certain distaste for the way in which she so shamelessly borrowed from others without attribution.

She held out to the listeners – or rather, to those of them still attending to her words (the Misses Antrobus had long since given up any pretence at being attentive, and were making faces at each other behind their mother's back when they believed they were unobserved) – if not an actual promise, at least a firm expectation of discovering treasure of some kind.

She explained some of the techniques of archaeology as she understood them, and the different techniques to discover objects that lurked in the soil.

"And finally," she concluded, making Robert Quantock sit up, "I propose that we all meet in front of The Hurst here tomorrow morning at nine o'clock, with trowels and a garden-sieve, and perhaps a rake. Pepino and I will provide the pegs and the tapes for marking out the site" (Pepino gave a slight start at this) "and we can spend the morning together happily discovering our past."

There was to be, it seemed, no performance of the 'Moonlight Sonata' which had been appropriated by her as her special piece, at least not for the masses, but as soon as the last guests (Mrs Weston in her bath-chair and Henry Luton) had left, Lucia seated herself at her piano, and while her right hand dripped triplets, her left provided the harmonies of the noble Beethoven. To a performance of this noble work by Lucia, the only permissible response, to be made by both performer and audience at the end of the performance, was a silence of a few seconds, to be followed by a soft sigh, optionally accompanied (chiefly in Lucia's case) by the application of the corner of a handkerchief to the eyes.

As the last notes died away, her head, silhouetted against the curtains, drooped, and she sighed, with her sigh accompanied in perfect time by those of Georgie and Pepino.

"And so, as the admirable Pepys says, to bed," Lucia commanded her men. "We must be ready to start at nine precisely."

Georgie coughed. "I think..." he began.

"Yes?"

"I think we should ask the farmer, Joe Martin, if we may dig in his field. It would be very embarrassing if he decided to turn us off. It is private land, after all."

Lucia's brows furrowed in thought. "I suppose you are right. Would you like to talk to him early tomorrow morning, Georgie?"

"Certainly not," he replied with some firmness. "I think either you or Pepino should talk to him."

"I think you should be the one to speak to him," Lucia's husband told her firmly. "He is almost certain to listen favourably to an appeal from you rather than from either me or Georgie."

"Oh, very well. How you work me," said Lucia. "But in that case, Georgie, you must come round here and help Pepino with the pegs and tapes."

Georgie agreed, and went home to the hot bath prepared for him by the admirable Foljambe. After his bath, he slipped happily into bed, having given instructions that he was to be woken half an hour earlier than usual, an dreamed of finding a beautiful golden statue of Apollo.

FIVE

The next morning saw the majority of the previous evening's guests assembled outside The Hurst, armed with a variety of garden implements. Robert Quantock had apparently decided to devote the morning to a study of Romanian oils, a subject that formed the source of much of the Quantocks' prosperity, and the Vicar had been called away unexpectedly to an old lady's bedside.

The morning had turned out to be a fine one, with a few clouds in a blue sky, and a gentle breeze which promised to cool the brows of those toiling in the pursuit of historical knowledge (and possibly of golden treasure).

Even Mrs Weston, grasping a large garden

rake in one hand, and a large sieve in the other, while seated in her bath-chair, propelled as always, by Henry Luton, and appearing to Georgie's eyes as a kind of bucolic Boadicea in her chariot, armed with spear and shield, seemed ready for the exercise.

Pepino and Georgie had rescued several yards of tape from the shed where it had been stored preparatory to marking out a tennis-court behind The Hurst, and armed with this and the pegs to hold it down, were at the head of the procession.

But Lucia was missing. Pepino explained to them all that she had gone over to see Mr Martin, the farmer, regarding permission to dig in his field. She had been gone since half-past eight o'clock, he told them, and so should therefore be expected back at any minute.

Sure enough at five minutes past nine, Lucia returned, smiling.

"Dear Mr Martin," she exclaimed. "He is very interested in what we may find under Long Meadow, but he explained that he must plant his seeds soon, and therefore we may only carry out our researches today and tomorrow."

This announcement came as a slight relief to Georgie, who was not anticipating many days of unending back-breaking work with any great degree of pleasure.

Lucia led her small army of archaeologists in procession to the Long Meadow, and then stopped at the gate.

"Where exactly did you discover your pieces of glass?" she asked, turning to Georgie.

"Over there," he replied, pointing to a spot only a few yards from the gate.

"Then that would seem to be the most likely spot to start," she declared. "Georgie and Pepino, you must use the tape and pegs to mark out a series of squares for us to excavate."

This work turned out to be rather tedious, since the soil had recently been turned by the plough, and although Georgie was protecting his hands with the gloves that he customarily used for gardening, and his feet with the oldest set of boots that he possessed, he regretted the morning's choice of jacket and trousers, which would require a good brushing by Foljambe when he returned. However, at length, this work of marking out the areas to be explored was accomplished, and Lucia apportioned her army into the resulting areas that had been marked off.

Georgie found himself paired with Daisy Quantock. Piggy Antrobus was with her sister and mother in an adjacent area. Colonel Boucher, fortified with moral assistance by Mrs Weston from her bath-chair, and more practically by Mrs Rumbold in another area, and Lucia and Pepino together in the last.

"How should we do this?" Daisy asked Georgie. "Shall I dig and you sieve, or the other way round?"

"I'll dig first," said Georgie, feeling rather noble.

"Or perhaps we could both dig together and then sieve together?" suggested Daisy.

"No, because then we wouldn't know who had found what," said Georgie. "Or where exactly things had been found. Lucia says that is a very important thing to remember."

He took his trowel and carefully started to clear away the top layer of soil that had been turned over by the plough. "Of course," he said, feeling that by now he was somewhat of an expert on this business, "the plough will have upset the layers, but we might be lucky and find something that the plough has turned up without having to dig deeply."

He filled a small bucket that he had brought with him with the soil, and took it to Daisy.

"How exciting," she said. "I wonder what you can have found."

Unfortunately, when they examined the contents of the sieve after shaking out the loose earth, the haul consisted of a few stones, a couple of earthworms, and a centipede, at the last of which Daisy let out a shriek, and Georgie was forced to empty the contents of the site at a safe distance, to prevent the return of the loathsome creature.

"Perhaps we'll be lucky next time," said Georgie, and cleared away another portion of the square. This time some fragments of iridescent glass appeared in the sieve along with the stones and the earthworms.

"Well, those do look pretty," Daisy told Georgie. "My turn."

She took over the trowel and started digging enthusiastically. After a few minutes, she gave a little cry, and stopped her excavation.

"What's the matter, Daisy?" asked Georgie. "Are you hurt?"

"No, no," she cried excitedly. "Look!" She pointed to the hole where she had been digging, which was now quite deep, and at the bottom of which a large square object was now uncovered. "A brick!"

"I don't think that's very special, is it?"

"But it might be a Roman brick," said Daisy. "Help me get it out."

Together, they excavated further, and discovered that it was not just one brick, but several, still cemented together, and of a very different type to the bricks that were typically to be found in Riseholme.

"I really do believe that you've discovered something Roman," said Georgie. "Well done." He and Daisy gently lifted the lump of bricks and mortar out of the ground and stepped back to admire it.

"Lucia!" called Daisy. "Look what we have found!"

Lucia put down her trowel and hurried over. "Roman, I fancy," she said, squinting through half-closed eyes to appraise the find. "Yes, definitely Roman. I think that shows that we are on the right track." She hurried back to her own square, where Pepino was busy separating stones and worms from the soil that he had just excavated.

The next "find" was that of Colonel Boucher, who came over to Georgie with some fragments of pottery in the palm of his hand.

"What do you make of these, then, Pillson?"

Georgie took them and examined one piece carefully. "They look a bit like pieces of flower pots to me," he said.

"That's what I thought at first as well, but

then I saw this." The Colonel held out his hand with a bigger fragment, on the surface of which was a relief pattern on what might have been vine leaves. "Now don't you go telling me that's a flower pot."

Georgie was forced to agree that this was no flower pot, and he remembered something he had read in the book he had lent to Lucia. "I believe that's known as Samian ware, Colonel," he said. "Who knows, you might find a whole bowl or vase or something, and I believe that would be very valuable."

"Well, then," replied the Colonel, and resumed his digging with new energy.

Returning to Daisy, Georgie found her busily engaged in excavating another large piece of brickwork.

"I don't think we should have taken out that first piece of brickwork," said Georgie, "and we should leave that piece in its place — oh, too late." Daisy had strained and struggled, and now triumphantly laid the lump of masonry on the side of the trench.

"What were you saying, Georgie?" she asked, mopping her round red face with a handkerchief.

"We should be leaving those pieces where they are so that we can determine what sort of building we are excavating." He examined the hole. "If you ask me, these walls that we have discovered are going to go under the hedge into the next field, and we don't have permission to dig there."

"Oh dear," said Daisy. "I suppose we could put them back."

"Too late for that now," said Georgie. "Let's carry on, but carefully. Maybe we will discover some lovely Samian ware like the fragments that Mrs Rumbold and the Colonel have found."

Alas, there was no Samian ware in the part of the field where Daisy and Georgie were digging, though Colonel Boucher and Mrs Rumbold continued to discover more shards of the red pottery, urged on my Mrs Weston, who operated the sieve from the comfort of her bath-chair while the others stooped and dug away enthusiastically.

After a few hours of exhausting digging and sifting, Georgie felt it was time for a break, and he stood up straight, his aching back protesting, and went over to Lucia.

"Any news?" he asked.

Lucia took this enquiry in the spirit in which it was intended, namely, a question as to whether she had discovered anything of interest.

"Nothing," she sighed. "I had no idea that there were so many worms and other crawling things in the soil, though."

Pepino, clearly glad of the interruption, ceased his digging, and sighed. "I think it is time for lunch," he said to Lucia.

"An excellent idea," said Georgie. "May I ask you and Lucia to take lunch with me? I have asked Foljambe to prepare a cold luncheon to be eaten outside."

"How considerate of you, Georgie. We won't have to change our clothes or our shoes if it is outside." She raised her voice. "I suggest that we all take lunch now, and reassemble at two o'clock, if that is convenient."

With sighs of relief, the diggers ceased their digging and the sievers ceased their sieving and the party broke up, returning to their different houses.

Foljambe, as requested, had prepared an excellent cold meal, which Georgie and his guests enjoyed as they sat under his fig-tree.

"We must dig faster," said Lucia through a mouthful of ham salad. "Just think, we have spent half a day, and all we have discovered are dear Daisy's bricks, and of course, they may not be Roman anyway."

"Oh, I believe they are Roman," said Georgie

loyally. "The shape and the size are not modern, anyway. And then there are those pieces of Samian ware which the Colonel and Mrs Rumbold found."

Lucia put her head on one side, and looked at Georgie quizzically. "Georgie, do you honestly believe those are Roman pottery, and not just some fragments of old flower pots?"

"Oh, certainly," he replied brightly. "There were some lovely pieces of relief moulding on them which I've never seen on any flower pot." He paused. "If I might make a suggestion..."

"Of course. After all, it was you who discovered the first pieces of glass," Lucia answered him generously.

"Very well, then. Daisy's bricks show us in which direction the Roman wall stretched—"

"If it really is Roman," Lucia sniffed.

"I think we can assume that it is," Georgie told her firmly. "And that means that we are digging in the wrong places. When we return, I think you and Pepino should move to another spot, and perhaps Mrs Antrobus and her daughters as well. Since Daisy and I have found a wall, there may well be other things in our little patch, and Colonel Boucher seems very happy with his pottery."

"That seems like a very sensible idea,"

observed Pepino, who had been getting a little tired of digging away and finding nothing except worms and various other creatures.

Lucia sighed. "Very possibly you are right, Georgie. When we have finished these delicious early strawberries – are they really from your own garden? – we shall return and do as you suggest."

Lucia explained the proposal to Piggy and Goosie, who relayed the idea into Mrs Antrobus's ear-trumpet, and new pegs and tapes were laid out.

Within ten minutes of digging resuming, Lucia gave a cry. "Georgie! Some Samian ware, I am sure. Come and look!"

Georgie trotted over obediently, and examined Lucia's finds with an eye that he hoped was critical.

"Yes, these look very much like the sort of thing that Colonel Boucher and the others have been discovering," he told her. He left her trying to fit together some pieces of what looked as though it might well have been a bowl.

On the next sieve of earth that Georgie dug out, a coin made its appearance. Encrusted with dirt as it was, it was impossible to make out to what century, or indeed, to what historical period, it belonged, but a brief immersion in a cup with which Georgie had thoughtfully provided himself together with a vacuum flask of cool water, revealed some details.

A head in profile, crowned with a laurel wreath caused Georgie's heart to skip a little, but the coin seemed to be a little too well preserved to be a Roman coin, and the inscription of "GEORGIUS II REX" left him in no doubt that it was a penny from the reign of the second Hanoverian monarch.

But it was left to Mrs Antrobus to make the best find of the day. Piggy and Goosie, perhaps lured by the promise of golden treasure, had been working hard at the digging, allowing their mother to sift through the soil in search of Roman relics.

"Well, I declare!" said Mrs Antrobus in stentorian tones. Everyone stopped what they were doing, and looked at her. "See here!" she exclaimed, waving aloft some small object that was invisible to her audience, who clustered around in an attempt to view her find. Nestling in her outstretched palm was what appeared to be a large safety-pin of an antique design, covered in mud.

Georgie quickly brought forward his cup that he had used to wash the coin, and after a little time, the object was revealed to be positively antique, and of a shape that Lucia instantly pronounced to be Roman. "It's a brooch, Mrs Antrobus," she shouted into the ear-trumpet. "What the Romans called a fibula."

"Well, I never!" said Piggy. "That's wonderful, mamma," and started skipping in glee. Goosie, not to be outdone, seized hold of her sister's hands, and they continued their pretty gambolling until Piggy's foot went into a freshly dug hole, and she stumbled.

"Well, I must say that is a most handsome find," said Daisy. "Not as big as my bricks, of course, but much more interesting, I suppose."

The discovery of the fibula spurred the other diggers to new flights of energy for the remaining part of the day, and though Georgie discovered more glass which he convinced himself was Roman, while Daisy found some earthenware which appeared to be part of a drain ("It's certain to be Roman" she said, "as nothing has been built here since then"), and Colonel Boucher carefully unearthed a nearly complete beautiful bowl of Samian ware, missing only one small piece to complete its perfection, Lucia and Pepino had evidently drawn the short straw and discovered nothing.

At length, the party collectively expressed

itself to be weary, and the members carefully packed up their tools and their finds.

"An excellent day," said Lucia to Georgie, as they walked across the green. "Tomorrow we shall find great things, I am sure, now that we know the lie of the land, so to speak."

SIX

However much treasure might originally have been anticipated, on the next day the band of archaeologists was reduced to three: namely, Lucia, Pepino, and Georgie. Indeed, when he awoke, Georgie was not sure that he would be able to get out of bed, the exercise of the previous day having left his muscles and joints aching. However, a restorative cup of tea provided by Foljambe, followed by a hot bath, allowed him to eat his breakfast in relative comfort, and by the time he had finished his last piece of toast, he felt ready to work on the Roman villa once more.

But sadly, when he reached Long Meadow, only Lucia and Pepino were to be seen.

"I am sure the others will arrive soon," Lucia said, but her words were far from prophetic, and the three of them started digging in silence, broken only by faint exclamations from Georgie as his back made its existence known to him once more, and by occasional tuts of disappointment from Lucia as another sieve-full of earth proved to contain nothing more than stones and worms.

Georgie was just about to call it a day, his back and shoulders doing their best to convince him of this decision, when Lucia gave a sudden cry.

"Georgie! Pepino! Look!"

She was crouched in the shallow hole where she and Pepino had been digging, and pointing to a piece of reddish pottery protruding from the earth.

"We must be very careful," she said. "This is undoubtedly Samian ware, and a beautiful shape – maybe some sort of vessel sacred to the gods." She delicately attacked the soil around the earthenware with her trowel to loosen it. At length she was able to free her prize from the clutches of the earth, and held aloft a good half of a large bowl.

"Do you have your water with you, Georgie, so that we may clean it somehow?" she asked.

"Maybe there is some decoration on it, such as Colonel Boucher discovered on his bowl?"

A careful cleaning of the bowl showed a frieze running around the outside of the bowl, beautifully decorated with figures and trees.

"How perfectly wonderful," said Georgie. "How clever of you to have found it."

"The other half must be here," said Lucia. "Pepino and Georgie, you must help me find it."

Alas, the other half of the bowl was probably to be found, but it was in unrecognisable fragments, most no larger than a half-crown, and Lucia despaired of ever being able to put them together to restore her find.

"Never mind," said Georgie. "Maybe some of the pieces you discovered yesterday might be part of the bowl. It could be like one of those puzzle things where a picture is cut into pieces and you have to put it back together again. Perfect for long winter evenings."

Lucia sighed. "I suppose so," she said. "Perhaps we should find all the parts we can, and then stop before the rain starts." She pointed to the west, where clouds were gathering in an otherwise blue sky, and Georgie guessed that Lucia, too, was somewhat tired of digging, but was unwilling to admit it.

The last twenty minutes turned up a few

more pieces of glass for Georgie, and some more fragments of Samian ware which Lucia added to her collection.

"There," she said, standing up somewhat painfully, as it seemed to Georgie. "You must allow us to give you lunch today, Georgie. I will take our finds back to The Hurst, and you and Pepino can remove and pack up the pegs and the tapes and fill in the holes that we have dug and so on."

It was half an hour after Lucia had departed the field that Pepino and Georgie finally came to the end of their tasks. As they started to leave, the farmer came up to meet them.

"Off then, are you?" he asked. "Nothing to be found, eh?"

"A few pieces of glass," said Georgie modestly, "and some pieces of old crockery." He did not feel it necessary to mention Mrs Antrobus's fibula.

"Reckon they're Roman, then?"

"Oh, I think so. Don't you agree?" he appealed to Pepino for confirmation.

"Oh yes, certainly Roman," said Pepino. "No doubt at all. Not valuable, except to a historian, of course, but extremely interesting."

"Thank you so much for allowing us to dig in your field."

Farmer Martin cast an approving eye over what had been until less than an hour previously an archaeological site. "You've left it neater than the moles would have done, I'll say that. Thank you for that. Next time I find a Roman temple or something like that I'll let you know, shall I?" He chuckled at his own wit.

"Oh, yes. Thank you. Please do," said Georgie, somewhat startled by this offer.

Pepino and Georgie made their way to The Hurst. Both were walking somewhat stiffly after the unaccustomed exercise they had taken, and gratefully set down their burdens of tools and tape and pegs at the entrance.

Lucia had not disappointed. Lunch was a hearty and nourishing meal of soup, followed by some cutlets, and a jam sponge pudding.

As he put down his spoon and fork, Pepino yawned. "I don't know about you, Georgie, or you, Lucia, but I must say that I feel more than a little tired."

Georgie yawned in sympathy. "Me too," he declared, emphatically, if not strictly grammatically.

"You men!" Lucia scoffed. "As for me, I feel fresh as a daisy."

"Speaking of daisies," said Georgie, "where

was she today? And the Antrobuses, and the Colonel and Mrs Weston?"

"I'm sure I don't know," Lucia sniffed. "I find it hard to believe that such a fascinating subject as our nation's history could fail to hold their interest."

"Perhaps I could drop in on Daisy on my way home," suggested Georgie, "and find out what is going on?"

"Yes, perhaps you could do that," Lucia agreed.

SEVEN

Accordingly, after lunch, Georgie made his way past Daisy's house, conveniently located next to his own, in the hope of seeing her or Robert in the garden. His hopes were fulfilled. Daisy was examining a large mulberry tree that had pride of place in her "little patch", as she sometimes referred to it.

"Any news?" she called out as Georgie stopped outside her gate. "I saw you and Lucia and Pepino going over to Long Meadow. Did you find anything?"

"Yes, Lucia found most of an almost undamaged Samian bowl. Beautiful decoration. But we missed you. Where were you?"

Daisy left her mulberry tree and came over

to the gate where Georgie was standing. "Just looking to see if we were going to get any mulberries," she said by way of explanation of what she had been doing. Without stopping for breath, she continued, "When I woke up this morning, I felt so stiff and sore that I really felt I couldn't do any more, just for a few old bricks and pieces of drain. And now that I've got them home, I really don't know what I am going to do with them. Robert says I should just bury them in the garden, but I don't really want to do that. What do you think?"

"I'm sure I don't know," said Georgie. "Hide them behind your garden shed, and something will come to mind soon, you can be certain."

"And," Daisy added almost breathlessly, "we have two visitors arriving tomorrow, and I need to prepare their rooms."

"Oh?" said Georgie. "Friends?"

"Well," Daisy answered him, "I suppose one of them is someone you wouldn't really call a friend, but Robert has done business with him in the past. He's a lawyer who has helped Robert from time to time, and he's meant to be frightfully clever. He's a Member of Parliament for somewhere in Wales as well, and Robert says that the Prime Minister speaks very well of him, and he may find a place in the Cabinet before long, though I wouldn't know about that. When he's settled here, perhaps you can all come round for dinner and meet him and his secretary, who is also coming to stay with him."

"That will be nice," said Georgie. "What's his name? The Member of Parliament's, I mean."

"Do you know, I don't believe I have heard his Christian name, but he is a Mr Griffiths. Never mind, as soon as he arrives, I shall find out exactly when and where he was born, and then I can send all of that off to Madame Evantis and I will know all about his future."

"It sounds terribly exciting," said Georgie, successfully stifling a yawn. "I shall look forward to meeting your Mr Griffiths."

Georgie returned to his house, and despite the hour, asked Foljambe to draw a bath for him, into which he slipped with pleasure, resting his aching back and limbs.

When he had relaxed, and re-dressed, he went downstairs to dust his bibelots in their special case, which even Foljambe was prohibited from touching, and which had been sadly neglected over the past couple of days.

When he had finished, he sat back in his favourite armchair and Foljambe brought him a cup of tea with a slice of seed cake.

"While you were in the bath, sir," she told him, "your sister Miss Hermione telephoned."

Georgie, who was fond of his sisters Hermione and Ursula, usually known as Hermy and Ursy, despite the fact that they were in so many ways his opposites, sighed. "Oh dear, does that mean that I must make a trunk call to telephone her?"

"Yes, sir, she asked you to return her call. She was very brief. She laughed when I told her that you were taking a bath, but she asked me to let you know that she and Miss Ursula will be visiting this part of the country soon, and she wished to know whether she and Miss Ursula could stay here."

"What day did she say they were planning to arrive? And how long are they intending to stay?"

"I'm afraid she did not say, sir."

"Very well. How tarsome." Georgie applied himself to the tedious task of placing a trunk call to his sister.

He quickly established that the dates that his sisters were planning to visit Riseholme included one for which he had planned a garden-party.

"Well, we wouldn't want to come to that," Hermy told him. "You'd only be cross with us anyway, because Ursy and I wouldn't be able to stop laughing at your Mrs Lucas. Can't you just put off your silly old garden-party to another day?"

"No, impossible," said Georgie, untruthfully. "I've already sent out all the invitations, and it's too late to change them all just for your convenience. And anyway, Mrs Quantock's got an important visitor coming – a Member of Parliament, Mr Griffiths. No, you don't want to come to my garden-party, and I am not going to put it off to another day." It was not as if Georgie was devoid of brotherly love, but Hermy and Ursy were at their best untidy and noisy, and at their worst dirty and boisterous, not only disturbing the spirit of calm and harmony that characterised Georgie's household, but also creating extra work for Foljambe, whom they despised as being haughty and overbearing.

"Well, we'll just have to find a ditch to sleep in, then, won't we, brother of mine?" said Hermy.

Georgie had a sudden thought. "How many nights are you thinking of staying? Three?"

"Yes."

"Then I'll reserve a room for two at the Crown in Brinton. I'll pay for you to have your dinner there, and your bed and breakfast."

"Well, that is kind of you, Georgie. Thank you so much." There was no trace of sarcasm in her voice. "Ursy and I will be drinking your health."

The conversation ended, and Georgie replaced the receiver.

"My sisters will not be staying here, Foljambe. I'm sure you will have enough to do preparing for the garden-party without any guests staying here."

"I'm sure you're right, sir. Thank you for letting me know."

Georgie picked up his petit point embroidery and started work on it. The evening was spent quietly with his cushion cover, and some quiet practice of the bass part of a Mozart quartet arranged for four hands on the piano, which he was sure Lucia would ask him to play in the coming days.

EIGHT

On awakening the next morning, Georgie discovered that his newspaper had not been delivered.

"I'll just go over to the newsagent's," he said to Foljambe after he had finished his breakfast, "and see what has happened to it."

It was a fine morning, but Georgie wrapped his throat carefully in a new scarlet muffler against the morning dews and damps as he set off across the green. On the way he noticed some workmen unloading various pieces of wood from a lorry.

"What's all this wood here?" he asked curiously.

"Well, sir, this is a job from Mrs Lucas over

the other side of the green," pointing to The Hurst. "She and her husband have bought all this from Littlethorpe down the way, and it's all to go here," pointing to a place by the duck-pond.

"I see," said Georgie. "But what is it?"

"When we've put it together again, sir, they say it will be some sort of stocks that they put you in when you did something bad, and all the folks used to come and laugh at you, and throw nasty things like rotten cabbages and the like at you. I learned about them at school, I did. And now they're to go here, Mr and Mrs Lucas tell me. Wonder who'll be the first one to be sitting in them, eh, sir?"

Georgie found himself laughing. "Oh, I am sure that no one in Riseholme will be using them," he said. "Thank you for telling me all about them," he added courteously (for Georgie was never anything but courteous) and walked on.

Now that he thought about it, he remembered Lucia and Pepino discussing the purchase of these stocks which they had seen in Littlethorpe, which the local parish council had decided were surplus to requirements, and which Lucia and Pepino intended to bring to Riseholme in order to increase the antiquity of the place. Already Lucia had ceased to refer to the patch of water in the green as the "duck-pond" and now referred to it as the "duck-ing-pond" in the presumed hope that those who heard it referred to as such would make an association with witchcraft trials and other picturesque forms of rude justice in days gone by.

He entered the newsagents and enquired after the fate of his paper. Alas, no copies of that particular journal had made their way to Riseholme that day, the proprietor explained apologetically. Georgie was forced to purchase an unfamiliar newspaper, which dealt with more political news than Georgie usually consumed. He tucked the rolled paper under his arm and walked back to his house.

As he passed The Hurst, Lucia called out to him. "*Georgino mio*! Have you seen on the green? Guess!"

"It's the stocks that you and Pepino bought from Littlethorpe. I've just been talking to the workmen," he told her.

If Lucia was disappointed in his prior knowledge of her secret, she hid it well. "Do you not agree that they will add an air of antiquity to the village?" Lucia enquired earnestly. "When the American visitors come to admire our little community, with the ducking-pond, and our sweet little houses, and the Ambermere Arms, they are sure to remark the ancient stocks, are they not? All a part of our island nation's rich history."

"Oh, certainly, certainly," said Georgie. While Lucia was speaking, he had been idly glancing at the newspaper in his hand. He noticed something that seemed familiar in one paragraph and he felt a need to go back to his house and digest it in peace.

"Ickle *musica* later?" asked Lucia, combining Italian with the baby-talk that she and Georgie used to carry on their innocent flirtation.

"Lovely," said Georgie, absently. He had just made the connection between the name he had just read and the conversation he had recently had with Daisy Quantock. "Yes," he said, feeling Lucia's sharp gaze upon him. "We must try that new Mozart. After lunch, perhaps?"

"That will be splendid. *Au reservoir.*"

Georgie was puzzled by that last phrase. He was sure that Lucia's French was more fluent than her last words would imply. Perhaps it was intended as some sort of joke or witticism. He would have to ask her.

"Goodbye," he said firmly. "Until after lunch, then," and returned to his house.

He immediately settled down in his armchair to read the newspaper article that had caught his eye. He had not been mistaken. The Honourable Member for Llanfair, Mr Erddig Griffiths, was reported as having made a speech in the House, which, according to the writer of the article, was sure to give him a place in the next Cabinet.

"So Daisy was right about him, then," Georgie said to himself. "I'm not very interested in law or that sort of thing, and I don't really know anything about politics, but it would be interesting to meet someone who did know about them." He took a pair of scissors from his needlework tray and carefully cut out the article, with the intention of showing it to Lucia at some time in the future.

So saying, he put down his newspaper and returned to his bibelots, many of which had been in his possession for a number of years now. The miniature porringer from the time of Queen Anne had a slight spot of tarnish on the handle, and he gently polished it away until it shone.

Before lunch he practiced the Mozart once more, confident that Lucia would be doing the same. He felt little shame in this, as in his eyes these two "cheats" cancelled each other out.

He set off for The Hurst after lunch, donning a somewhat daring new jacket of a shade of light blue of which he was particularly fond, matching it with a cravat of a slightly more intense blue. To his intense pleasure, Lucia noticed it at once.

"My dear!" she exclaimed on beholding his finery. "How perfectly splendid, and how well it becomes you. Is oo ready for ickle morsel of Mozartino?"

Georgie nodded, and they took their places at the piano stool. Georgie, as usual, took the bass part, and Lucia carried the tune in the treble. They contrived to make their way through the piece without too much obvious stumbling, and though both strongly suspected the other of having practised the piece in advance, neither would break the etiquette of their musical intimacy by accusing the other. At the end of the piece, they applauded each other, as was their custom, with Pepino, who had been reclining on a sofa behind them, applauding both equally. In keeping with tradition, Georgie slipped off the piano stool, taking his place beside Pepino, as Lucia re-seated herself and started to play the opening triplets of the slow movement of Beethoven's 'Moonlight Sonata'.

The piece having drawn to a close, the ritual

silence having been observed, and the customary sighs duly having been given, Lucia turned to Georgie. "Any news?" she asked him. "Since this morning, I mean."

"Daisy Quantock is having a visitor to stay," Georgie told her.

"Dear Daisy? And who is this visitor? Madame Sclerosis or some such name? The one who tells her about what the stars and planets have in store for us?"

"No, apparently he's a Member of Parliament, and he is staying with his secretary."

"Really?" said Lucia in some surprise. "Which party does he stand for?"

This was something that Georgie had not discovered, but he put a brave face on it, and told Lucia that Mr Erddig Griffiths was a lawyer, and represented Llanfair in Wales.

It was not for Lucia to cavil about lawyers, given her husband's occupation, but she still found it necessary to find some way of disparaging Daisy Quantock's find. "Oh, Wales," Lucia sniffed audibly, and with that sniff consigned the land of bards and Owen Glendower to the outer darkness. "He probably has Socialist tendencies. Still, he may have some good qualities, otherwise I do not suppose they would allow him to be elected."

Georgie was far from being convinced that this was the way in which British democracy worked, but he held his peace.

"I suppose he may be a very decent kind of person, relatively speaking," Lucia went on. Pepino, we should invite him to tea, perhaps? And maybe dinner after a few days?"

"Oh, quite, quite," said Pepino, who gave a slight start on hearing himself addressed.

"When does he arrive?" Lucia asked Georgie.

"Tomorrow, I believe," he said. "There was something about him in the newspaper this morning." Georgie produced the article that he had cut from the paper earlier, and presented it to Lucia.

She read it, her eyebrows arched in surprise at some passages, and she wordlessly handed it to Pepino. "Well?" she asked her husband, when he had clearly finished reading it.

"The writer here clearly says that 'he is a man to watch'," Pepino answered.

"Well, if Daisy invites us to meet him, or if he accepts our invitation, then we will have plenty of opportunity to do that, won't we?" said Lucia brightly.

NINE

Georgie was proved correct about the arrival of Daisy and Robert's guest, when a taxi drew up outside the Quantocks' house the next day and disgorged a quantity of luggage, followed by two middle-aged men, dressed in what Georgie thought of as "London suits".

One of these was tall and walked with an air of confidence towards the gate, followed by his companion, who was considerably shorter and with an almost dishevelled appearance.

"The Member of Parliament followed by his secretary," Georgie thought to himself. "Highly distinguished, to be sure."

Despite his intense curiosity, he decided that he would wait until Daisy invited him to meet

Mr Griffiths rather than forcing himself on her and her visitors. Even so, he hoped that his invitation would come before one was issued to Lucia, thereby allowing him to be the one to inform her of the details of this new and exciting visitor to Riseholme.

With that happy thought in his mind, Georgie set off across the green, and without obviously angling for any invitation, ensured that he was clearly visible from the Quantocks' front windows as he made his way towards the haberdashers-cum-drapers, where he was intending to choose some silk for his latest piece of petit point embroidery.

On the way, he passed Mrs Weston, being wheeled in her bath-chair at what seemed to Georgie to be a terrifying speed.

"Good morning, Mrs Weston," he greeted her, tipping his hat to her. "I must say, that does look rather dangerous, going so fast like that. Suppose you hit a stone or something like that?"

"Nonsense," said Mrs Weston firmly. "Henry's very good about that sort of thing, aren't you, Henry? You must inherit it from your mother, who's always been so good and careful. When she's cutting up the fish, I have to say that it makes me nervous to watch her filleting the haddock when I go there. 'Aren't you worried, Mrs Luton?' I said to her one day when I went there for a nice bit of halibut for my supper, because I always say there's nothing better than halibut for supper unless it's turbot, and you can't always get turbot for some reason I don't know. Perhaps they migrate like swallows or hibernate like hedgehogs or something. Anyway, she told me she wasn't worried at all and the secret, she told me, was always to have the sharpest knife you could, and that's because it never slips and cuts you, so there." She paused for breath. "Any news?"

"Yes. Daisy Quantock's got a visitor."

"Two visitors, surely?" Mrs Weston, like all true Riseholmeites, took a keen and lively interest in the doings of her neighbours. "I saw them arrive in that taxi that comes from Brinton. "And it was just after ten o'clock that I saw them, because the church clock had struck the hour about five minutes before and that's always three minutes fast by the grandfather clock in my hall, and I know that's right because Mr Weston paid a lot for it in that shop in Brinton by the butcher's that closed last year where you could get the best lamb chops I have ever tasted. And when I talked to the Vicar here about it he said that it meant that people came to church early and weren't late and I've never heard of such a thing in my life. 'Vicar,' I said to him, because that's what I call him, I could never get used to calling him Reverend Rumbold, or Mr Rumbold, 'Vicar, that's playing with God's time and you should be ashamed of yourself for doing it.' And do you know, he just laughed at me and said that the idea of time was a human concept and that clocks were not important. Well, I ask you." She paused. "Who were the visitors, do you know?"

"I know who one of them is, and I can guess the other. The tall man is Mr Erddig Griffiths, the Member of Parliament, and the other is his secretary. Daisy Quantock told me that Mr Griffiths and his secretary were coming to stay with them. Apparently Mr Griffiths is a lawyer, and he has worked together with Robert on some business."

"Well, I must say, that is interesting," said Mrs Weston. "Do you think we'll be invited to meet him?"

"I'm sure we will," said Georgie.

"And what does Lucia have to say about all this?" asked Mrs Weston.

"I don't think she's found out all about Mr Griffiths yet," Georgie said.

"Well, that will be a nice surprise, won't it?" said Mrs Weston.

"Yes, indeed," said Georgie. "Now I really must get on." He left, listening to Mrs Weston's instructions to Henry Luton to start pushing the bath-chair at high speed.

He passed the Ambermere Arms, which in addition to its primary function as an inn, also made available for sale certain traditional items of furniture and other knick-knacks, many of which had been in the possession of the proprietor for several weeks following their purchase from antique shops in other parts of the country. American visitors especially were taken by the idea that a genuine (or as near genuine as made little visible difference) table from the time of Charles II which had graced the entrance hall of the indisputably ancient Ambermere Arms from time immemorial – that is to say, since before their arrival in Riseholme – could now, for a relatively modest outlay, adorn a room on the other side of the Atlantic.

Not only furniture, but other smaller items often found their way into the Ambermere Arms, and from there, one or two had quietly migrated into Georgie's collection of bibelots. Naturally, he took care not to have these items

on display so soon after their recent sojourn
at the Arms, but allowed them a decent period
of acclimatisation before their introduction to
the public – or at any rate, those members of
the public privileged enough to be allowed to
gaze on them.

He arrived at the draper's, and took his time
selecting exactly the right shade of puce to
complete his cushion-cover. Naturally, it was
necessary for him to examine the different silks
by daylight, and this kept him moving to the
door of the shop, yarn in hand, and although
keeping one eye on the silk, he kept observing
the doings on the green, especially those connected with the Quantocks, whose operations
were of special interest.

As he watched, the Misses Antrobus emerged,
and went over to the workman who was install-
ing Lucia's stocks next to the pond, and who
now seemed to have almost completed his task.
Even from this distance, Georgie could hear
the excited girlish squeals of Piggy and Goosie
as they gambolled around him.

He had just made his final decision on the
yarn when he noticed the front door of the
Quantocks' house open, and Daisy appeared
with the taller of her visitors – the Member of
Parliament. She was pointing at the different

houses and buildings surrounding the green, including Georgie's own house, and The Hurst, Lucia and Pepino's residence. Her guest tipped his hat to Daisy, and set off down the garden path, clearly (at least it was clear to Georgie) intending to take a tour of the green, and discover Riseholme and its charms.

Much as he would have liked to act as a tourist guide to the visitor, Georgie was somewhat shy regarding the idea of forcing himself (as he saw it) on the Member for Llanfair. However, he calculated that if he set off promptly and walked at a good speed, he would intercept Daisy's guest approximately in front of The Hurst, where he would be able to raise his hat and politely enquire after the visitor's health.

With that in mind, he left the draper's, claiming an unspecified urgent appointment, and promising to return soon for the yarn. As he had calculated, he approached the stranger at a point where Lucia, should she be watching from the window (and he hoped that she would be) would witness his meeting.

"Good morning, sir," he greeted the other as they came closer. "A beautiful morning, is it not?"

"Indeed it is," replied the visitor, raising his hat in return. "And a most beautiful spot in which to live, if I may say so." His voice was rich and well-rounded – the voice of a born orator, Georgie thought to himself, as Erddig Griffiths had been described in the newspaper article. "May I ask if you yourself live here, Mr er..?"

"Pillson," replied Georgie. "George Pillson." They shook hands, but the stranger did not introduce himself, presumably having assumed, with the wisdom that comes of political experience, that his hostess had probably introduced him already in absentia. "Yes, I moved here some years ago. I live in the house next to Mr and Mrs Quantock with whom I believe you are staying."

"Indeed we are. I trust we will have the pleasure of your company soon." He made a slight bow, and was on his way.

Georgie, greatly excited, made up his mind to visit Lucia with the news.

TEN

"Who was that I saw talking with you?" asked Lucia as Georgie was shown into the drawing-room, where she might have been suspected by the uncharitable of having been secretly engaged with a popular novel, the cover of which could be seen coyly nestling under a cushion, rather than studying the life of Beethoven which she was holding. Georgie noticed that the latter was upside-down, but tactfully held his peace.

"I believe that to be Mr Erddig Griffiths," said Georgie. "The Member for Llanfair."

"I see," said Lucia reflectively. "I must say, he seems a very decent sort of person. Not at all what I would have expected from reading about him in the newspapers."

"He was very polite," Georgie informed her. "He hoped that we – that is, he and I – would meet again at the Quantocks."

"And did he ask about The Hurst and about who lives here?" Lucia asked eagerly.

Georgie was forced to reply that he had made no such enquiry.

"Never mind," said Lucia, and there was a small note of disappointment in her voice. "Dear Daisy perhaps forgot to mention that there was a fellow member of the Bar in residence in Riseholme."

"No doubt that is it," said Georgie, though he remained a little puzzled as to why Daisy should ever do such a thing.

"I shall go over and leave Pepino's and my cards after lunch," Lucia declared. "It may well be that he and Pepino are members of the same Inn of Court. At any rate, they are bound to reply to such an approach."

Alas for Lucia. The two cards were duly left, but by tea-time, no reply of any kind had appeared. Nor, although Lucia was expecting a reply at any moment, was a reply or even an acknowledgement seemingly forthcoming that evening, or indeed, at any time.

"I cannot believe that even dear Daisy, with all her failings, would be so petty," she remarked.

Pepino, who was as anxious to meet this much-lauded politician as his wife, though managing to conceal it more effectively, replied to her complaint. "No doubt they are unused to our Riseholme standards of courtesy," he remarked. "You must recall that while we were in London, matters were much more informal and the social niceties as we expect to observe here were often neglected. Besides," he said as he continued to consider the matter, "it is quite possible that Mr Griffiths has come here for a working holiday, and will have no time for social intercourse, which he might consider to be frivolous and beneath his notice."

"But I was not intending to undertake any such social intercourse, as you put it. If I meet a man – or a woman, I may add – who has achieved distinction in a particular field, it is not my desire to make idle chit-chat with them. Rather, I wish to sit at their feet and ask questions – the Socratic method, you know – and learn from the wisdom of their replies."

"I am sure you are right," Pepino assured her, "and nothing could be more noble or high-minded. But how is Mr Griffiths to know of this?"

"I would have thought Daisy Quantock could have let him know. Or if she is too wrapped up in her star-gazing to care about her neighbours' welfare, then Robert could have mentioned it to his guests."

"No doubt you are right, dear," Pepino remarked.

"In any case, I shall follow Georgie's example of this morning, and make a point of greeting him if he ventures out into the village again."

Despite Lucia's constant vigilance as she sat by the window with a book in her hand (the popular novel, alas, rather than the life of Beethoven) scanning the green for the Member, the next day brought no invitation, and no sign of Mr Griffiths, though the elderly secretary could be seen making his way to the Ambermere Arms in the early evening.

"I am surprised that a respected Member of Parliament should employ a secretary who drinks in a public house," she said to Georgie, who had come round to play duets.

"I don't really see that it's any business of ours," Georgie told her. "In any case, you and I have both been known to take a glass of wine from time to time, haven't we?"

"That is true," Lucia admitted. "But we do not feel the need to go into a common taproom in order to indulge our appetites, do we?" She fixed Georgie with her sharp dark eyes.

"Very true," said Georgie, though what business it was of Lucia's when and where people enjoyed a drink was beyond him.

"So, from the pettiness of today's doings, to noble Beethoven," said Lucia, opening her music. "'Awakening of cheerful feelings on arrival in the countryside'. Is that not a splendid theme for a symphony? Me to take tweble? Bass part looks awful diffy for poor Lucia. Oo to take firm bass, and oo must not scold poor Lucia too hard when she goes wrong. Ready? *Uno, duo, tre.*" And they were off.

Following a satisfactory performance of the first movement of the 'Pastoral' symphony, in which Lucia only broke down twice, and Georgie once, the usual performance of the first movement of the 'Moonlight' took place. On this occasion, the silence was shorter than usual, and the sighs perhaps a little less heartfelt as Lucia turned to gaze out of the window.

"It seems like a beautiful evening for a walk around the green," she announced. "I will just get my hat and coat and take a stroll. No, sweet of you both to ask, but I shall be perfectly happy by myself."

As she left the room, Georgie moved to the

window, from where he saw his previous in-
terlocutor emerging from Daisy Quantock's
garden. Lucia was already heading across the
green on a course that promised to intersect
with that of the visitor, and her intention was
plain to him. Pepino rose from his seat and
joined him, and after he had looked out of the
window, the two men exchanged a silent look,
in Pepino's case accompanied by a faint half-
smile, an expression which Georgie felt it inappropriate to return.

They watched intently as the distance between Lucia and her prey decreased to the
point where they both stopped, and it was
clear that a few words were exchanged. After
a short while, the visitor continued, and Lucia
turned back towards The Hurst. Georgie and
Pepino returned to their seats, and were busily engaged in conversation when Lucia re-en-
tered the room.

"Such a polite man," were her words on entering the room. "I happened to come across dear
Daisy's visitor, and I have to say that he seemed
to be a most civil and courteous man, as you
said, Georgie. I really cannot understand how
our cards have been ignored. However, when
I asked him to tea some day soon, he – most
politely, I must say – regretted that it would

not be possible, and said 'we are engaged in highly important and confidential Government work' and would have little time for social visits." She sniffed. "I suppose that by 'we' he is referring to himself and his secretary, since I do not see dear Daisy or Robert being engaged on that sort of matter. One quite wonders why he has come to Riseholme at all if he does not intend to take advantage of our society, which, if I may say so, is quite the intellectual and cultural equal of any in London."

"Oh quite," agreed Georgie.

"And furthermore, there are none of those tedious distractions that Londoners seem to find so important. The new play that everyone must see, the gossip about some of the most scandalous personalities that one can imagine, and some of the most ghastly paintings and exhibitions. No, when I think of our sweet little Riseholme, and our duets together, the charming little watercolours that you produce, Georgie, and Pepino's prose poems, not to mention the whole village steeped in the time of Shakespeare and his Anne. And of course, our glorious Roman past. No, no, London is not for us any more, is it, Pepino? Or for you, Georgie."

Georgie was aware that an outburst of this

kind from Lucia was very often a prelude to
a course of action that required justification.
And so it proved to be in this case.

"And so," Lucia concluded, "if Mr Erddig
Griffiths has determined that Riseholme and
its inhabitants are not for him, then at least
one of these inhabitants, that is to say myself,
cannot make time for him. He does not exist in
my eyes."

And so it proved to be. For the remainder of
the fortnight during which Mr Griffiths and
his secretary stayed with the Quantocks (the
length of the stay exciting some comment from
the Riseholmeites), if Lucia chanced to meet
either of the visitors, she simply passed them
by as if they were invisible. Truly, they did not
exist for her, and several times when she met
Daisy, she successfully managed to forget that
Daisy had guests staying with her when she
issued invitations to dinner, or to a musical
evening at The Hurst – invitations which were
invariably turned down by the Quantocks.

However, Lucia could hardly complain of dis-
crimination against her and Pepino. Despite
the hope expressed to Georgie that he would
meet the visitors at the Quantocks', no invitation was issued to him, nor to the Antrobuses
("but who would want a Member of Parliament

to meet Piggy and Goosie?" he asked himself).
Colonel Boucher and Mrs Weston were like-
wise deprived of the pleasure of the company
of Mr Erddig Griffiths, MP.

ELEVEN

It must not be supposed that on the whole, the inhabitants of Riseholme felt themselves to be unduly "put upon", as Mrs Weston's maid, Elizabeth, would have expressed it. Engaging in Parliamentary politics, after all, was a pursuit fit only for those who had made their choice to reside in London, and had little better to occupy their time.

The members of Riseholme society, though they might deplore the Quantocks' behaviour in the hoarding of their guests, nonetheless heaved secret sighs of relief that they would not have to ensure endless lectures on the bimetallic question or the importance of battle-cruisers in the naval estimates for the coming year – topics which they were sure would be the principal subjects of conversation were they to be invited to meet Mr Griffiths and his secretary.

It was true that Colonel Boucher had on one occasion found himself in the Ambermere Arms at the same time as the visitor who had been identified by Georgie as the secretary of Mr Griffiths, who was sitting in a corner of the saloon bar, nursing what appeared to be a small whisky and soda, and apparently listening to the other conversations in the bar as if, as the Colonel put it, "the dashed man was some sort of foreign spy or someone come here to steal our secrets".

Though it had initially been Colonel Boucher's intention to strike up a conversation with the stranger and introduce himself, there was something in the other's countenance that precluded any attempts at intimacy, and the Colonel retired without having acknowledged the other's presence, or indeed, having been himself acknowledged.

On another occasion, the Member for Llanfair was seen with Robert Quantock. Both were carrying a bag of golf-clubs, and walking in the direction of the links, so the purpose of their walk seemed apparent. Although they passed within hailing distance of Mrs Weston and Colonel Boucher, who were engaged in conversation on the green, neither of the golfers seemed to see fit to greet or even to acknowledge the presence of the Riseholmeites. As if to make up for their silence, Mrs Weston had a great deal to say on the subject later on when she met Georgie.

Meanwhile, Lucia was engaged in various projects. She had set herself to learn a Bach fugue, but found that it was beyond the capability of one pair of hands – at least if that pair was hers – to play it, and she enrolled Georgie to assist her. The resulting sound was quite attractive, and Pepino was moved to applaud and praise them both with "*Brava! Bravo!*" in the most correct Italian at the end of their unveiling to him of the results of their practice.

Georgie worked on his petit point, and on his charming cushion cover, and in the end was pleased enough with it to assign it a place in his pretty little drawing-room.

"Well, that is very nice and pretty, sir," Foljambe told him when she first saw it in its intended position. "And if I may say so, sir, there's not that many gentlemen who could produce such a thing."

"Why, thank you, Foljambe," Georgie

replied, somewhat flattered by this opinion of Foljambe's.

Mrs Weston, as might have been expected, was somewhat scathing about the whole affair of the Member for Llanfair.

"I'm sure I don't know why Robert and Daisy Quantock are behaving the way they are," she said to Georgie one day. "If I had the Prince of Wales staying with me, I declare that I would allow all my friends to come and meet him. 'Important government business' indeed! Why, Mr Weston was an alderman before we came to Riseholme, and I can tell you that being an alderman is a lot more difficult than being a Member of Parliament. There are more than five hundred of them, and only ten aldermen in our city, so that makes fifty times more work for each of them if you take the trouble to think about it. No, if you want my opinion," and here she dropped her voice, "it's all to do with that stars and planets business she was so keen on before the visitors arrived. When they've gone, we'll be told that it was because Venus was in the wrong place, or the Scorpion had bitten the Twins or something like that, and so it wouldn't be suitable. Just a lot of folderol and superstition, if you ask me. Now my aunt was so superstitious that she hardly ever went outside. Maybe there was a ladder that she had to walk under to reach the shops, or she had seen the new moon in a mirror or something of that sort. 'Jane,' she used to say to me. 'Jane, I can't go down to the butcher's today because I've seen a black cat. So would you go down and ask him for a nice piece of lamb's liver.' Of course, it wasn't always a black cat that she'd seen. Once she got a terrible shock and had to stay in her bed for two days because she thought she'd seen a ghost in the mirror, and it was only her dressing-gown hanging on the back of the bedroom door. But you and I, we don't believe in ghosts, do we, Mr Georgie?"

"Certainly not," said Georgie firmly, though he wasn't quite sure whether he did or not.

"Piggy saw a ghost once," said Goosie Antrobus. The two young Antrobuses had approached, unobserved by either Georgie or Mrs Weston.

"Silly," replied Piggy. "I never really thought it was a ghost."

"Yes you did," said her sister. "You screamed and screamed and I had to give you some sal volatile to keep you quiet."

"That was because I hit my toe."

"Wasn't."

"Was, silly."

"Stop it, you two," said Mrs Weston firmly. Other than their mother, Mrs Weston was the only other person in Riseholme who seemed to have any control over them. Even Lucia often seemed powerless to control their girlish spirits. They subsided, and Mrs Weston continued.

"As I was saying, I think that Daisy Quantock has her head full of that rubbish, and I'm not ashamed to call it rubbish, about the stars and the planets and everything, and that's why she hasn't asked any of us to meet her guests, but she's too embarrassed to admit it. And that's just like my aunt, who'd stay in her bed if she thought there was something that was going to cause trouble later in the day, but if anyone asked for her it was always 'I've got a touch of a cold and I'm not getting out of bed for anyone'."

Mrs Antrobus, who had come up and heard the last sentence through her ear-trumpet, broke in. "I'm sorry to hear you have a cold, Mrs Weston. You should be in bed with a hot water bottle and some honey and lemon."

Georgie vainly tried to explain to her that it was not Mrs Weston who had a cold, and indeed, it was not even her aunt who had suffered, but it was a difficult task, and eventually he gave up the attempt.

The parliament on the green was on the

point of breaking up, but at that moment Lady Ambermere's motor appeared on the other side of the road and pulled up outside the Quantocks' house. All eyes were fixed upon it as Lady Ambermere herself, followed by Pug, the Ambermere dog, borne in the arms of Miss Lyall, her companion, swept through the gate which had been held open for her by her chauffeur.

It seemed that she was expected, as the door opened before Lady Ambermere even reached it, and she, Pug, and Miss Lyall were admitted to the house.

Mrs Weston, the three Antrobuses, and Georgie observed all this, turned to look at each other, and turned back once more to gaze at the now closed front door of the Quantock house.

"Well!" said Mrs Weston and Georgie together. There wasn't much more that could be said, but there was plenty of food for thought which required time for digestion before it could be fully appreciated.

As for Mrs Antrobus and her daughters, they were struck dumb by this development, Mrs Antrobus only exclaiming, "I never would have believed it of them."

The meeting then proceeded to carry out its

original intention of breaking up. Mrs Weston giving orders to Henry Luton to take her to Colonel Boucher's house, the Antrobuses set off for home, and Georgie hurried over to The Hurst to inform Lucia and Pepino of these latest dastardly developments.

"Any news?" Lucia asked him when he was admitted, slightly out of breath, to the garden where Lucia and Pepino were sitting on the bench in the resting place which bade visitors to 'Bide a wee'.

"Guess," said Georgie in the best Riseholme manner.

"The Prime Minister has visited dear Daisy, but we're not allowed to see him or meet him?" said Lucia.

"You are nearly right," Georgie told her. "Lady Ambermere just walked into the house," he told Lucia and Pepino, who were hanging on every word. "She didn't even have to knock. The door was opened for her as she walked up the garden path."

"Well!" exclaimed Lucia, just as Georgie and Mrs Weston had done earlier.

"And," Georgie went on, "Pug and Miss Lyall also went in."

Lucia laughed. "I am sure Mr Griffiths will be charmed by those visitors," she said. "Let us hope that Pug does not bite him. I must say, I am surprised at Daisy and Robert's behaviour."

"It may not be her choice, carissima," Pepino interjected. "It is quite likely that Mr Griffiths is busy with government business, as he claims, and does not wish to see anyone from Riseholme."

"But Lady Ambermere?" asked Lucia, incredulously.

"The late Lord Ambermere was very important in politics," Pepino explained, "and it may be that Lady Ambermere still has some influence in areas where Mr Griffiths has an interest."

"And Pug, too?" Lucia enquired sarcastically. "I am sure Mr Griffiths will be fascinated to learn Pug's views on the League of Nations and the bimetallic question. And Miss Lyall, too. Her views on universal female suffrage will no doubt change the government's views on the matter. No, I am afraid that dear Daisy has proved herself to be nothing more or less than a snob, as they say."

Whatever differing opinions Pepino and Georgie held on the subject were left unexpressed, and the conversation took a new turn, as if the previous subject had not been introduced at all.

"I have been reading," Lucia began, in a lofty tone, so unlike her usual conversational manner, "about the wonderful creatures that used to roam this earth. Such majestic beasts, and such majestic names. Brontosaurus, the thunder lizard, from the Greek, you know, or Tyrannosaurus Rex, the tyrant king lizard. Such power, such majesty! I believe we owe it to ourselves and to future generations to discover these magnificent creatures."

"Surely they all died out millions and millions of years ago," objected Georgie. "Surely you don't expect to go into Newcombe Woods and find a brontosaurus eating the trees there?"

Lucia laughed her silvery laugh. "No, of course not," she said. "No, I have fossils in mind. The quarry near the road to Littlethorpe would be an excellent place to look, I feel."

It says much for Lucia's powers of persuasion and self-confidence that neither her husband nor Georgie ever even thought of questioning her judgement on the matter.

TWELVE

The day following the visit of the Ambermere party to the Quantocks saw the departure of Mr Erddig Griffiths and his secretary. Whether there was a link between the visit and the departure, as Mrs Weston suggested, the presence of Lady Ambermere having persuaded the Member for Llanfair that Riseholme was not as pleasant a place as he had previously believed, or whether this had been planned in advance, no-one ever discovered. For Daisy, despite broad hints being placed in her conversational path over which she must leap in order to carry the conversation forward, simply ignored and side-stepped these fences, and talked instead about the magnificent crop of mulberries she expected to see in the autumn.

In any event, Mr Griffiths and the unnamed secretary were observed stepping into a Brinton taxicab at thirty-seven minutes past nine precisely, according to Mrs Weston.

"And that will allow them to catch the ten past ten express to London," she told Colonel Boucher. "That was always the train that Mr Weston used to take whenever he went to London, which he had to do sometimes on account of business. He never told me what kind of business it was, but some days he would open the post, and look at a letter and say to me, 'Jane, I'm going to have to catch the ten minutes past ten train from Brinton to London today. I shall be back in time for dinner.' And do you know, he always was, except for one time when I waited dinner for him until half-past nine and he never came back. So I sat up and worried about him, and bless me, he came in through the door at half past one in the morning. Now some might say that he'd been drinking and missed his train, and had to come on later, but it wasn't anything like that at all. He told me that the engine driver had had some sort of funny turn as they were driving along and had to stop the train in the middle of a field somewhere for several hours. Well, it sounded so strange that I just had to ask someone, and they told me that it was all perfectly true, so there.

"Anyway," she continued, "maybe we will see Robert and Daisy Quantock again, after they've shut themselves up away from us for so long, but why they think they're so much better than us that we're not allowed to meet their guests, I'm sure I don't know."

Indeed, Daisy was to be seen on the green, all smiles, for the first time since her visitors had arrived. However, much as she may have been expecting a rush of eager enquiries as to her health, her doings, and the nature and conduct of her recent visitors, no one approached her. It was clearly up to her to make the first moves, and to repair the lines of communication which she had so obviously and inadvertently destroyed. She retired to the safety of her house, and waited until she saw her next-door neighbour, Georgie, at work in his garden (her bedroom gave an excellent view of Georgie's garden as well as her own) and made her way downstairs and out into her own garden in order to meet him by chance.

"Any news?" she asked, in the familiar Riseholme greeting.

Georgie was taken aback by what he saw as the effrontery of this greeting. It was Daisy, after all, who had had the opportunity of creating news by extending invitations to meet Mr Griffiths and his secretary, and had deprived the whole of Riseholme of the opportunity of enjoyably, if not altogether productively, discussing these visitors.

"Oh, nothing much," he said. "My roses have got greenfly."

"So have mine," said Daisy. "Madame Evantis says that's the influence of Saturn." She paused. "Though I am not so sure about her these days. It seems to me that she makes up a lot of what she says." The next words came out in a rush, as if she was worried about how they would be received. "Mr Griffiths thinks it is all nonsense. I asked him if he would like Madame to cast his horoscope, and he was quite rude when he refused. I found out later from his secretary that Mr Griffiths is a member of some Welsh non-Conformist denomination, which disapproves of things like that." She laughed. "I don't think that he disapproves of alcohol, like some of them, though." She dropped her voice, though no one else was within earshot. "Two bottles of wine each evening at dinner between the four of us, and I can tell you that I only had one glass, and Robert two at the most. The rest..." That was interesting enough, but she continued. "And he went off to the Ambermere Arms in the evenings quite a few times as well. 'Observing the population,' he called it. Hmph. Observing the bottom of a glass of whisky, if the smell was anything to go by."

"The secretary?"

"No, no, Mr Griffiths. Mr Beedle, the secretary, always stayed with us. A most amusing and intelligent young man, I must say, but he spent most of his evenings working on government business for Mr Griffiths."

"I beg your pardon?" Georgie answered, more than a little confused by this last. "Who went to the Ambermere Arms? Not the secretary, but Mr Griffiths, the Member for Llanfair?"

"That's right," said Daisy brightly.

"So..." Georgie was assembling the pieces of the puzzle in his head. "So Mr Griffiths was the older, shorter man, and the secretary, Mr Beedle, was it? was the taller younger man?"

"Of course."

This gave Georgie considerable pause for thought. "I think I should tell you," he said at length, "that we were all convinced that Mr Griffiths was the secretary and your Mr Beedle was the Member of Parliament." He grasped the nettle. "Why on earth didn't you invite us all to meet him? We would have all enjoyed what he had to say."

This placed Daisy Quantock in a quandary. If she were to repeat what the Member of Llanfair had said about the inhabitants of Riseholme, and indeed, about Riseholme itself, she would be accused (unjustly, since they were not words that she had actually uttered) of treason towards the village and her neighbours. "He was busy with government work," she said after a short pause, "and felt he could not spare the time."

"I see," said Georgie, though he was attempting to reconcile the urgent press of government business with the visits to the Ambermere Arms. "Well, we would naturally have respected his wishes in that regard, but it is unfortunate that we were unable to meet him."

They parted on that note, Daisy with a vague feeling of disloyalty towards her friends and neighbours, and Georgie bursting with the news of the true identity of Daisy's guests.

Lucia was the first to know of Georgie's discovery, and she burst into a peal of merry laughter.

"Just fancy, Georgie," she said. "You thought

he was the Member of Parliament, and he was only the secretary! How comic."

Georgie was more than a little nettled by this. "So did you," he pointed out.

"Only following your example," Lucia replied after a moment's thought. She observed Georgie's face, which had set in lines of resentment, and relented almost instantly. "Oo mustn't be cwoss," she cooed in baby-talk. "Lucia only having ickle joke."

"Not funny," said Georgie. But then a thought struck him, and he started to smile. "But Colonel Boucher mistook the MP for his secretary in the Ambermere Arms. Now, that is somewhat amusing, though I doubt if the Colonel would find it so."

Lucia smiled. "And dear Daisy's comments about Mr Griffiths not wanting to interrupt his government business." She shook her head. "Such a clumsy way of evading the truth."

"And what is the truth, then?" asked Georgie.

"Who knows? Who cares? For my part, I shall simply pretend that the last two weeks have not happened, at least as far as Daisy and Robert and her visitor – whatever his name is. You see, I have forgotten already. He is as nothing to me." And Lucia seemed to hold in her hand what might have been an imaginary dandelion head, and blew it away.

"And now?" said Georgie.

"Fossils await us," said Lucia. "Now that Daisy has so kindly consented to re-join us, we can all make our way to the old quarry tomorrow or the next day and start our researches."

THIRTEEN

As before, Georgie was appointed by Lucia as her recruiting sergeant, going round the houses of Riseholme. Rather than going to the Quantocks first, since he was unsure as to whether Lucia wanted them to be included in the expedition, he started with Mrs Antrobus, and as he had feared, Piggy and Goosie were enthusiastic about the project.

"Piggy will come and give you a hand if you get stuck," Goosie told him and giggled as girlishly as only a thirty-year old can giggle.

"And Goosie will come and give us both a hand if we can't dig up a fossil," Piggy told Georgie, putting a hand on Georgie's sleeve, much to his annoyance. He suspected jam, but would have to wait until he left the Antrobuses before he could check his new jacket for marks and stains.

"And you should wear older clothes. You might get dirty," he told them.

"Oh that doesn't matter," said Goosie. "We're used to being dirty."

"Speak for yourself," said her sister, and slapped Goosie's hand playfully.

"I was speaking for both of us," said Goosie, and slapped back.

"Girls, girls," bellowed Mrs Antrobus, and there was relative calm.

Mrs Weston, when he visited her, announced to Georgie that she would not be taking part in the expedition. "I saw all the dinosaurs that I ever want to see when I was a girl," she said. "It was at the Crystal Palace and in the park nearby they have statues of them. I was only nine years old – no, I must have been ten, because my family had moved to Grafton Square when I was nine, and I definitely remember going back to the Grafton Square house after we'd seen the dinosaurs. We had three large steps going up to the front door and I used to count them, and my bedroom looked out of the back of the house, and I remember lying in bed and wondering if a dinosaur was going to come in in the night and eat me up, because when I first saw one of those models in the Crystal Palace, it gave me quite a turn. My mother said that I started crying, though I don't remember that. Anyway, I've seen all the dinosaurs in my life that I ever want to see, and I don't think I would be able to go to the quarry in my bathchair anyway."

Colonel Boucher was quite enthusiastic, having come away from the Roman excavation with some tangible results. "Bless me, that Roman stuff was hard work," he said. "But worth the trouble," indicating the pieces of Samian ware that now occupied a prominent position in his cabinet. "Well worth it. And if we can find some things as good as those, then I'm all for it. When do we start?"

The Vicar and Mrs Rumbold informed Georgie that they were otherwise engaged for the next day, and apologised profusely for being unable to join the party.

After what he considered to have been a good morning's work, Georgie happily trotted over to The Hurst to tell Lucia the news. He found her deep in the encyclopaedia, engaged in the study of fossils.

"Georgino," she said to him excitedly. "I never knew there were so many things in the earth, or under it, I should say. Look here." She pointed to an illustration in the book.

After examining the picture briefly, Georgie gave his opinion. "It looks perfectly foul," he said. "What is it?"

"It's called a trilobite," Lucia told him. "At one time, they were almost the only creatures living on the earth, or rather, in the sea."

He looked a little closer. "Perhaps you could make trilobite *à la Riseholme* with it," he suggested. "It does look a little like a lobster."

He said this in such a serious tone that Lucia looked at him with concern. "Georgie," she said in a tone of voice that expressed concern. "These creatures died out many millions of years ago." She then noticed the smile spreading over his face and laughed. "Oh, Georgie, fancy your saying that! Oh dear. I almost believed you for an instant."

"Do you think we'll find any of these things tomorrow?"

"Who knows? I confess that these things are very difficult to understand. I've been reading about all the different ages and periods and so on, and it's impossible to remember what comes when, or when the different creatures all lived. All these names. Trilobites were before dinosaurs, I am sure, but it's all so complicated. I think we will just have to take our hammers and see what we can find."

"It should be exciting, anyway," said Georgie. "Even if all we find are some of these trilobite things."

"There are lots of other things as well," said Lucia. "Look here."

"Oh, those are a lot prettier. What are they called?" asked Georgie.

"These are ammonites. It says they were a sort of shell, a bit like a snail."

"I hope we will find some of those."

"I also." She glanced at the clock on the mantelpiece. "Georgie, will you do something for poor ickle me?"

"Yes," he answered, but guardedly.

"You were so good at persuading people to join us on our Roman expedition. I know that you might think it strange after the way they have behaved, but could you please talk to the Quantocks about us all discovering the treasures of the past together? Prego."

"I don't know if I would call those trilobite things a 'treasure', but I can certainly do what you ask. Do you really want me to invite Daisy and Robert?"

"Of course. The events of the last two weeks have no meaning for me. I shall ignore them and Mr Griffiths, and that ridiculous secretary of his, setting himself up to be his master."

"Very well then. Goodbye."

"*Au reservoir.*"

Georgie stopped. "Don't you mean '*au revoir*'?" he asked.

"Georgie, it's ickle joke," she said in baby talk. "Just like your trilobite *à la Riseholme.*"

"Oh, I see. Very witty, now I see. *Au reservoir* to you, as well, then."

"Well, it does sound a bit interesting," Daisy admitted when Georgie informed her of the plans. "I must admit that I have been rather disappointed in Madame's predictions recently. She told me that only last week I would come into a great sum of money. Well, I did find a half-crown under the bed yesterday which Mr Griffiths must have dropped, but I don't think anyone would really call that a great sum of money, do you?"

"Maybe you'll find a rare fossil or something, and it will be worth a lot of money," said Georgie. "Or a new sort of dinosaur and they'll name it after you."

"That would be nice," said Daisy. "I'm sure there were lots and lots of different kinds of dinosaurs, and they don't know all of them yet. Anyway, how do we go about finding them?"

Georgie had been well briefed on the subject by Lucia, so he was able to answer this question readily.

"Well, it might be rather dusty and dirty," he said, "and we might need to go climbing over rocks and things at the quarry, so it's probably a good idea to wear clothes that aren't too smart."

"Like the ones I wear when I'm doing the garden?"

"Just like that," he told her.

"And do we just pick up these fossils?" Lucia had walked to the quarry to inspect the site, and had told Georgie what to expect.

"They're sort of stuck in the rock, rather like plums in a pudding. We'll each need a hammer and a chisel to get them out. And a stout basket to carry them in after we've found them. And maybe a brush like a paintbrush to clean the dust off the fossils when we've found them."

"I see," said Daisy. "It does sound a little like hard work. When will we be starting?"

"We will all meet on the green by the pond at nine o'clock tomorrow."

FOURTEEN

The Riseholme fossil hunting expedition gathered the next day at the appointed time, and presented an unusual aspect to those who usually saw the members in their usual costume. While Georgie and Daisy wore their gardening clothes, which in Georgie's case comprised of a pair of dark brown moleskin trousers and a Fair Isle pullover (how he wished he had worn them on the first day of the Roman 'dig'), and in Daisy's a very old cotton frock, whose best days were long behind it, Lucia was smartly and rather daringly arrayed in a short light blue outfit. Pepino was wearing a one-piece garment, similar to that worn by motor mechanics, and appeared to be quite at ease in it. The other members of the party were dressed oddly, if appropriately, and they provided a source of quiet amusement to the shopkeepers and other inhabitants of the village as Lucia led them on their way to the quarry, with hammers, chisels, brushes and baskets to hand.

Once at the quarry, Lucia, who had previously ascertained that there would be no workmen there that day, divided her party around the quarry.

Piggy and Goosie enthusiastically attacked the soft rock with their hammers, giggling and skipping around as they did so. Colonel Boucher was, as one might expect, somewhat more methodical, and before long he was able to claim the first find – an ammonite.

The others crowded round to admire and envy it, and to congratulate him on his find before returning to their own patches with renewed hopes and expectations. Piggy and Goosie were the next to find a fossil, but in their girlish over-enthusiasm they managed to break it into many pieces, and spent the next thirty minutes blaming each other for the mishap.

In the meantime, their mother had taken up Piggy's hammer and had carefully dislodged another fine ammonite which was duly admired by all except her daughters, who were still squabbling about their broken find.

Georgie had failed to discover any trilobites or ammonites, let alone a brontosaurus of his own, but he had extracted from the chalky sides of the quarry a number of curiously shaped flints, which he showed to Lucia.

"Not fossils, certainly," said Lucia. "I wonder if they might be prehistoric spear heads or arrowheads."

Pepino had joined them, and he gravely gave his opinion. "I believe those are stones which have been artificially shaped some thousands of years ago by our ancestors," he said. "Of course, I am no expert, but I feel that this is the case here."

Though his first instinct had been to throw them away, Georgie decided to keep the flints. They would seem to be considerably older than anything else in his bibelot cabinet, including the fragments of possibly Roman glass which now occupied a space there, but at the same time, they could hardly be classed as decorative.

Daisy (Robert had once again declared his disinclination to dig for ancient remains) had been patiently attacking a more remote part of the quarry. At times she gave a little cry, which the others took to mean either that she had either discovered an item of interest, or that she had hit her thumb with the hammer.

However, when Lucia had decided that the time had come for lunch, it was Daisy who presented a basket with at least half a dozen fine fossils of ammonites, at least two of which were really quite impressive.

"How marvellous," said Georgie, picking them up and examining them. "They are really most splendid."

"Better than my poor effort," said Colonel Boucher, who had failed to discover any more fossils after his first success.

On account of her deafness, Mrs Antrobus had failed to understand completely what had been going on, but her two daughters girlishly gambolled in front of Daisy in a vain attempt to secure some of her finds for themselves.

"No," said Daisy firmly, covering her basket with one hand and using the other to slap Piggy's hand, which was attempting to make its way into the basket and out again with an ammonite in its grasp. "I found them, and I am keeping them."

The Misses Antrobus retired disappointed, as Lucia and Pepino made their way to Daisy.

"Dear Daisy," said Lucia. "Such beautiful little fossils, aren't they?"

Daisy was justifiably annoyed at the adjective 'little'. The largest of her finds was at least twice as big as any other that had been discovered that day. "Thank you, Lucia," she smiled through gritted teeth. "And so many of them."

Lucia had no easy answer to that, but merely smiled and picked up her empty basket and turned for home.

When the expedition all reassembled after lunch, there seemed to be a renewed sense of purpose. Daisy's finds had established that there were indeed fossils to be discovered, of a size and number and quality that far surpassed most expectations. Piggy and Goosie were still convinced that the stony remains of some hitherto unknown large reptile lay waiting to be discovered, and they hammered and chipped away enthusiastically, waiting for the Piggysaurus or Goosiesaurus to reveal itself.

Georgie, somewhat to his relief, discovered no trilobites, but he did unearth an ammonite equalling the Colonel's in size and quality, though it fell short of Daisy's finest specimen in both respects. He also discovered a rather delicate fossil of a fern, which to his mind was more impressive than an ammonite.

Much to everyone's relief, though, Lucia's hard work in supervising Pepino was rewarded when a large ammonite appeared, and she carefully set about removing it from its setting with Pepino's aid.

All in all, the little party had discovered between them a considerable number of fossil ammonites, a fern, several interesting flints, and what Lucia insisted was a fossilised shark's tooth, though to Georgie's eye it appeared to be a curiously shaped stone.

"Alas, no dinosaurs," she complained to Pepino and Georgie as they made their way across the green, bearing their spoils.

A motor stood outside the Ambermere Arms, which Georgie recognised as the Brinton taxi.

"Look, they're unloading some luggage from it. I wonder who might be staying there."

Though the Ambermere Arms indeed provided lodgings, the majority of its business consisted of serving lunch (or in some cases, dinner) to the passengers of charabancs on their way to or from Stratford-upon-Avon. Visitors making more than an overnight stay, as Georgie had rather cleverly deduced from the size and number of the cases being unloaded, were uncommon.

The little party moved on to their respective

homes, and Georgie carefully deposited his finds in the hallway.

"These are not to be touched by anyone except me," he told Foljambe.

"Very good, sir. If you don't mind my saying so, they do look a little muddy. Might I take them through to the scullery for you?"

"Oh, yes, yes," said Georgie vaguely. He had just noticed through the window Daisy Quantock waving from her garden, and he hurried out to speak with her over the hedge.

"Any news?" he asked, already knowing that the answer would be in the affirmative.

"Yes, yes," Daisy said excitedly. "There's a new guest staying at the Ambermere Arms."

"I saw that."

"Yes, but do you know who it is?"

"No. Do you?"

"She comes from Tilling on the south coast. I know because I walked past and I caught sight of one of the luggage tickets on her suitcase. No sign of her though."

"And I suppose you know how long she's staying?" Georgie was being as sarcastic as he ever dared to be, but Daisy had an answer for him.

"Just over a week. I heard the taxi-driver say to her, 'I'll be seeing you a week on Tuesday then, Miss Mapp' as he drove away. And he didn't look too happy about it. She probably didn't tip him properly.

"So she's Miss Mapp, then?" said Georgie. "Alone?"

"I think so," said Daisy.

"And what does she look like?" Georgie asked.

"Oh, I never actually saw her. I heard the taxi driver call out to her, but she was in the Ambermere Arms, and I couldn't go peering in to look at her, could I?"

"I wonder what sort of person she is. Do you think she's the sort of person one could invite to tea?" said Georgie. He liked meeting new people and enlarging his circle of pleasant acquaintances. There was the additional bonus that should she turn out to be someone important or 'interesting', he would have stolen some sort of march on Lucia, and though this was not a principle that ruled his life, it nonetheless formed a pleasing prospect.

"We shall find out," said Daisy confidently. "I've just sent Robert to the Arms to buy some Madeira. He can ask the landlord about her."

As it happened, Robert came into his garden at that moment. "How did you get on with your digging today?" he asked Georgie. "Daisy came back with a load of old rubbish, if you ask me."

"They're not rubbish," said Daisy crossly. "They're important scientific specimens."

"And where are these important scientific specimens to live, then?" asked Robert.

"Oh, I don't know. Somewhere," Daisy said vaguely.

"Well, I didn't find as many as Daisy did. I did find a very pretty fern, though," Georgie told Robert in an attempt to lighten the mood.

"Anyway," said Daisy, her hands on her hips. "Who is she?"

Robert shrugged. "She's from Tilling..." he began.

"We knew that," said Daisy.

"...and she is staying for a little more than a week..." Robert went on as if he had not been interrupted.

"We knew that as well."

"And her name is Elizabeth Mapp. M A double P. I saw her name in the register."

"And she's on her own?" asked Daisy greedily.

"I'm sure I don't know for sure, but 'Elizabeth Mapp' was the only name in the register. So I think we can assume she's on her own." Robert Quantock could be very sarcastic at times.

"So you didn't see her?" Daisy asked, obviously disappointed.

"No, I believe she was in her bedroom, and I was not invited to join her there."

At this, Daisy said nothing, but put her hands on her hips and positively glared at her husband.

"Well, I'm sure we will meet her soon. I must be going," said Georgie, finding himself somewhat de trop. As he started to say goodbye, the French phrase in his mind revived an associated memory. "*Au reservoir*," he called out gaily.

"What was that?" Daisy asked him.

"Oh, it's Lucia's phrase. A joke," Georgie explained. "Like *au revoir*," he added, in case Daisy hadn't understood. She could sometimes be slow at seeing the point of jests and jokes.

"Oh, I see. I think I like it," Daisy told him. "*Au reservoir*."

FIFTEEN

On the following day, Georgie, smartly dressed in his second-best blazer and summer trousers, visited the Ambermere Arms for the express purpose of discovering more about Elizabeth Mapp. To accomplish this, he had become very interested in a Victorian oak settle which the landlord had purchased from a cottage in the next village, and was attempting to sell to American tourists as a Jacobean piece on which might have rested the royal rump of Charles I when he was fleeing the Parliamentarians.

To Georgie, whom he knew well, the settle was being presented in its true colours, and at a price which was totally unconnected to royalty. As it happened, Georgie was indeed in search of a handsome piece to adorn his entrance hall, and accordingly a modicum of honesty existed on both sides of the bargain.

In fact, Georgie had almost made up his mind to purchase the piece, and was bending to examine the lower portions in order to ensure that there was no woodworm or other sign of habitation by unwanted creatures, when he became aware of another person making their way along the passageway towards him.

As he glanced in the direction of the approaching footsteps, he saw someone who could only be the hitherto unobserved Elizabeth Mapp. As she drew nearer, she appeared to fill the whole corridor, and Georgie hastily scrambled to his feet to avoid the possibility of being crushed beneath what appeared to him to be an approaching juggernaut.

It was she who spoke first. "I am so terribly sorry to disturb you," she said, with a great smile which revealed a row of shining white teeth.

"Oh no, not at all," Georgie replied politely. "I was only looking at this," indicating the settle, "and wondering whether it would suit the other pieces in my hallway."

"It certainly would seem to harmonise with a

certain style of decoration," she answered, after appearing to consider the item. "It wouldn't do for me, of course."

"Oh?" Georgie enquired.

"My house is from the time of Queen Anne. A perfect little gem, you know, and introducing that settle, lovely as it might be, into it, would be a complete disaster. Complete," she repeated with emphasis.

"I see," said Georgie. "And may I ask where this delightful residence may be, Mrs. ...?" Although he already knew that Miss Mapp hailed from Tilling, he felt that this was a most ingenious method of extracting information, from the horse's mouth as it were. The expression seemed especially appropriate as she opened her mouth to reply, displaying those splendid teeth once more.

"Miss Elizabeth Mapp," was the reply. "From Tilling, in Sussex." There was a slight emphasis on the first word.

Georgie bowed slightly. "Georgie Pillson," he replied.

"And are you staying here, too?" asked Miss Mapp, a large white hand vaguely indicating the interior of the Ambermere Arms.

Georgie laughed. "No, no. I live there," he said, pointing to his house across the green.

"Oh, how charmingly quaint," was the reply. "This is your family's home? How fortunate you are to live in such a perfect little village as this. Of course, I would miss the marshes and the sea if I were to live inland – Tilling has the most glorious views, you know – but of course, we must consider that we all have different tastes." Though unexpressed explicitly, the clear implication of her words seemed to be that her taste was superior to those of others.

"Yes indeed," Georgie replied politely.

"And of course, the feeling of space. Your little house seems to be admirable in shape and form, but don't you find it just a teeny – shall we say, cramped?"

Georgie, who often regretted the lack of a separate room for his piano and his bibelots, indignantly replied, "Certainly not."

"Oh, do forgive me. I suppose when one lives in such a splendid house as I have the privilege to inhabit, one always makes comparisons." She turned her gaze to the other houses on the green.

"And who lives in those charming little cottages?" she asked, pointing to The Hurst.

Georgie explained that rather than being

three separate dwellings, these buildings in fact comprised one house.

"I see," said Miss Mapp. Her tone seemed to hold a tinge of disappointment that the people of Riseholme possessed houses that might begin to compete in size with those of Tilling. "And that there?"

"Colonel Boucher lives there."

"Indeed, a colonel? One of my neighbours, indeed, we are so close I might almost call him a friend, is a Major Benjy – I should rather say Major Flint," she corrected herself with a giggle. "He was in India for many years. Was your Colonel in India?"

"He was, but he hardly ever talks about it," said Georgie. This was not true – the Colonel, especially after a glass or two of wine, could and did discourse on his time in India for a number of hours.

"How delightful it is to find a native of this place who can tell me these things about the residents here," Miss Mapp said. "I realise that it would be a terrible imposition on your time, Mr Pillson, but do you think that you would be kind enough to show me around Riseholme at some point in my visit? I hardly dare take the liberty of asking, but..."

If Miss Mapp had been a few years younger,

Georgie would have described her as "smiling coquettishly". As it was, her smile as she entreated him reminded him powerfully of what he believed a tiger's expression to be on beholding the next course of its dinner. Even so, the chance of discovering more about this visitor to Riseholme before anyone else had the chance to do so was a powerful incentive for him to agree to the proposal. Although it was clear to Georgie that Miss Elizabeth Mapp was nowhere close to Mr Erddig Griffiths when it came to a place in national importance, it would be pleasant to know more than Daisy Quantock with regard to this latest visitor, and to release the information in grudging dribbles.

"I'd be delighted to show you around the village now, if you are free," he told her.

"Oh, how very kind of you to take pity on a poor stranger," she positively cooed.

They set off together, with Miss Mapp seeming to positively hang on Georgie's every word as he explained how Riseholme, far from being a rustic out-of-the-way village, was in fact a hive of artistic activity, with literature, theatre, music, and painting being the favoured arts.

"How charming and delightful," was her reaction. "Who would have thought that such things would exist here? Tilling, as you probably know, enjoys an enviable reputation for its refinement and culture. I confess to being something of a dabbler in watercolours myself. In fact, I am on the Hanging Committee of our local Art Society, which has done me the honour of electing me as President, and we hold an annual exhibition in our historic town hall. And music, you say? I am very partial to music myself – Mallards, my Queen Anne home, holds within its walls a very fine Blumenfelt piano which belonged to my Aunt Caroline."

"And you play?" enquired Georgie.

"Alas, no. So busy, you understand, with my painting, and my sweet flowers – Mallards has a beautiful garden from which I am supplied with flowers for my garden-room, and vegetables and fruit for my kitchen."

They walked on for a while without speaking, with Miss Mapp breaking the silence. "You mentioned theatrical performances, Mr Pillson. Surely there is no theatre here?" She gave a gay little laugh in order to demonstrate the absurdity of such a notion.

"Of course not," Georgie replied, a little crossly. "I was referring to our little gatherings where we often present plays, with ourselves as actors."

"Oh, I understand," with a brittle laugh. "And what sort of plays do you perform?"

"Our last production was the Scottish play – *Macbeth*, you know. Of course, we had to take many parts each, which was a strain on our memories, and hard work, but even so, it was most enjoyable."

Indeed, Lucia, who had acted not only as Lady Macbeth, First Witch, and Banquo's wife, but also as director, costume designer and stage manager, had worked them all to the point of near-exhaustion. However, in a review of the performance printed in the local Brinton newspaper, her sleep-walking scene as Lady Macbeth had been hailed as a triumph of the dramatic art. It must be admitted, though, that this review had largely been based on Lucia's own report of the performance which she had submitted to the paper (although only Georgie was aware of the full extent of this).

His own contribution, as Duncan and Macduff, not to mention the Third Witch (Daisy Quantock taking the parts of the Second Witch and the various female servants), had also been mentioned, and the adjective "regal" still rang in his ears when he recollected the review of his performance as the murdered king.

"How very brave of you to tackle Shakespeare," she commented. "Whoever would have believed it? And you, I take it, are the guiding spirit in all of this?"

Here Georgie was forced to utter a denial, and Lucia (though naturally Georgie referred to her as "Mrs Lucas") was introduced into the conversation as a subject. "It is she who owns those cottages that have been converted into a cottage," he told her. "And she is a most remarkable lady. Music, painting, literature, and Italian, you know."

"Indeed?" said Miss Mapp, with what seemed to be an expression of interest, though Georgie was a little unsure of the emphasis she had placed on that single word. "And who," she asked, with an alacrity that made it seem as though she was keen to change the subject of the conversation, are the Ambermeres, at whose Arms I am now staying?"

"Lord Ambermere died some years ago," Georgie explained, "and Lady Ambermere lives nearby. Sometimes she visits Riseholme with her companion, Miss Lyall, whom I see there. She is alone today, however. I must go and meet her." He indicated a thin stick-like figure some hundred yards away, and he turned his steps, and those of Miss Mapp, in that general direction.

"And how delightful to see you here, Miss Lyall," he said to her as he approached, Miss Mapp inn tow. "I see that the sun is shining in honour of your visit to Riseholme." It was his custom to make some sort of mild joke to her, of the kind that would bring a faint flush of colour to her cheeks, and exclaim, as she did now, "Oh, Mr Pillson!"

"And pray present my compliments to her ladyship when you return to the Hall."

"Certainly," answered the poor downtrodden Miss Lyall, entering the cart like a hip-bath that was provided for her use when running errands. Georgie gallantly passed up her basket containing her purchases from the greengrocer's, which brought another blush and an embarrassed word of thanks before she set off.

"You are acquainted with Lady Ambermere, then?" asked Miss Mapp, who had been discreetly following him, and who had observed the scene with some interest.

"I have a distant family connection to the late Lord Ambermere," Georgie told her. The news did not appear to be instantly welcome to Miss Mapp. Georgie, sensitive as he was to others' moods, attempted to make amends. "May I ask if you have anything planned for Saturday afternoon? Because if you have not, I am giving a small garden-party from two o'clock onward, and will be delighted to welcome you as my guest there."

Miss Mapp smiled, once again displaying an array of shining white teeth ("Like a hyaena," Georgie thought to himself). "With the greatest of pleasure," she told him.

"Excellent," he replied. "A breeze of fresh air into our stuffy old Riseholme," though it was hard to imagine anything much less breeze-like than Miss Elizabeth Mapp. They walked on together in the direction of The Hurst, where Georgie could see Lucia busily engaged working in her front garden.

As they drew nearer, Georgie observed Lucia looking up from her labours and noticing their approach.

"*Buon giorno*, Georgino," she trilled. "And a good morning to you..."

"Mapp. Elizabeth Mapp," delivered with a shining smile and display of those amazing teeth.

"Emmeline Lucas," was the reply.

"Ah, Mr Pillson has just been telling me about your success with Macbeth."

"Has he, indeed? I fear he is much too kind

about my poor efforts." Lucia paused. "Are you staying with us here in Riseholme for long?"

"Alas, a week only."

"But you will be here on Saturday afternoon?" Lucia demanded. "If so, I do hope that Georgie Pillson here has invited you to his garden-party then."

"I have indeed," said Georgie, "and Miss Mapp has very graciously accepted my invitation."

"Such an honour and a pleasure to be invited," simpered Miss Mapp.

SIXTEEN

Saturday morning dawned. As Georgie gazed out of the window, the blue sky and bright sunshine seemed to promise a beautiful afternoon for his garden-party. He had sent out the invitations two days previously, bearing the legend "Titum" on the top corner, thereby signifying that the occasion, though not of the highest social importance, nonetheless demanded a certain standard of dress from those attending. "Hitum" was the highest level on this scale, followed by "Titum", with "Scrub" indicating everyday wear. These were designations of Lucia's invention, which had been seized upon and used by the whole of Riseholme society.

He had not bothered to mention the presence of Miss Elizabeth Mapp at the party on the invitations – Lucia would, she knew, have taken care of that chore for him. He had been in two minds as to whether she should have invited Lady Ambermere, but eventually had decided against it. Lady Ambermere was inclined to patronise others, and Lucia had a violent dislike of being patronised. Also, if Lady Ambermere were to attend, Miss Lyall and her dog Pug would also have to attend, and though Georgie had no particular objection to Miss Lyall, Pug was inclined to make his way underfoot, and leave half-masticated portions of food, or worse, in his wake. In addition, Colonel Boucher was quite likely to bring his bulldogs with him, and there had been incidents in the past when Pug and these bulldogs had expressed differences of opinion.

Accordingly, even though Miss Mapp had ever so delicately hinted to Georgie that she would like to meet Lady Ambermere, he was in no mood to grant her that request. Elizabeth Mapp was to meet those members of Riseholme society who had been chosen by Georgie, and that was to be an end of it.

The time of the party arrived, with Elizabeth Mapp being the first to arrive, clad in a dress which seemed to be, to Georgie's far from in-expert eye, too young for her matronly figure, though it might have been appropriate at some time in the past.

"How good of you to take pity on a poor stranger in your midst, Mr Pillson. So kind and generous of you," she simpered.

"Not at all," replied Georgie. "Do take a seat and tell me if you are still enjoying your stay here?"

"Oh yes, indeed. Thanks to your showing me some of the sights and telling me about what goes on here, I've been able to make little expeditions on my own and find out more about this dear little place all on my own, and I have made one or two little piccies – watercolours, you know – that will create quite a stir when I show them to our Art Society in Tilling. I have to say, that you all sound as though you are terribly busy, but if I could just take a teensy peek at some of your paintings, which I am sure are perfect masterpieces when compared to my poor little efforts..." She let her voice trail off in a hopeful manner.

"Oh, I am sure that is not true," said Georgie. "But some time before you leave Riseholme I will be happy to let you see some of my poor efforts. But I forget myself. Tea, Miss Mapp? Milk and sugar?"

"Thank you. Most kind. Milk and four sugars if you would be so kind. A sweet tooth, you know." This little speech was accompanied by a smile displaying an array of ivory, but left unanswered the question as to which tooth was the one designated as being 'sweet'.

Georgie passed the order to Foljambe, who hastened to the tea-urn where quantities of 'the cup that cheers but does not inebriate' were waiting.

"Salmon and cucumber, and egg and cress. How you spoil your guests, Mr Pillson," said the guest, taking two or three of each kind.

"Ah, Colonel," said Georgie as he spotted two bulldogs rounding the corner, which invariably presaged the arrival of Colonel Boucher. He introduced him to Miss Mapp, and left Foljambe to provide him with refreshment.

The next to arrive were Lucia and her husband, a worried look on her face. It was a little unlike Lucia to arrive so early at a function. Typically, she was the last to arrive, ensuring that the gathering would be waiting for her to sweep in, at which point the festivities would be permitted to begin.

"*Georgino mio,*" she said on his greeting.

"Something terrible has happened. Perfectly awful."

"How tarsome. Does it concern *Hamlet*?" he asked, referring to the Shakespearian production that Lucia was arranging for the winter, rehearsals for which were about to start in a few weeks' time.

"No, no." She shook her head. "If it had concerned *Hamlet*, I am sure I could have managed better. Look." She reached into her bag and produced an article cut from a newspaper.

Georgie took it and read it, a look of horror spreading over his face. "It's Daisy's guest, Mr Erddig Griffiths, isn't it? He's just been appointed to one of the top positions in the Cabinet. Oh dear, and we weren't very polite to him, were we? I thought he was the other one's secretary, didn't I? Oh dear, oh dear, Lucia."

"And I followed your lead," Lucia added, somewhat crossly. "And we both cut him when we met him on the green, didn't we?"

"What will Daisy say?" asked Georgie. "And what will we be able to say to her? I'm sure I don't know," Georgie said.

"But we will soon find out. Here she comes with Robert," Lucia said.

Lucia decided to take the bull by the horns. "Dear Daisy," she greeted her. "Georgie's just been telling me all about your Mr Griffin who came to stay with you. He seems to have done rather well for himself."

"Mr Erddig Griffiths, not Griffin, dear Lucia, has indeed been made a member of the Privy Council and now holds a very distinguished post in the government."

"How nice for you," Lucia said. "To think that we had in the midst of our humble little Riseholme such a great man."

By this time Daisy was glad that she had not "shared" Mr Erddig Griffiths with Lucia. Had she done so, Lucia would by now have taken all the credit for his political elevation and referred to him as her exclusive property. As it was, there was no way she could make any such claim. "Quite so." Her tone was so aggressively neutral as to be positively hostile.

"And will you be visiting him in London?" asked Georgie, innocently.

"Yes," smiled Daisy. "We received a letter from him yesterday, was it not, Robert?"

"The day before," Robert corrected her.

"So it was. The day before. And in his letter, he let us know that he was to be made a Privy Councillor, and that we are invited to the ceremony confirming this to be held next month, as his guests."

"How nice for you, dear," said Lucia through clenched teeth. Why, oh why, had she believed Georgie's identification of Daisy's two guests, and why had she followed his lead in snubbing them? Miss Mapp was indeed a mere minnow compared to the whale of Mr Griffiths (though one might be forgiven an opposing opinion if bodily appearance was to be taken into account). She watched as Georgie introduced Daisy and Robert to the minnow, and left them comparing the relative advantages of Riseholme and Tilling.

Piggy and Goosie Antrobus came gambolling up to Georgie, holding hands and giggling girlishly. "Mamma told us that you were expecting a visitor. Is it that Mr Griffiths who stayed with the Quantocks, and who was in the newspaper this morning?"

"No, it is not," Georgie said, annoyed. "Miss Mapp from Tilling, who is staying at the Ambermere Arms, has been kind enough to come to my little gathering. Now do run along like good girls, and ask Foljambe to give you some tea. Ah, Mrs Antrobus," she said raising her voice and speaking directly into the large ear-trumpet which was presented to her.

"Is he here?" Mrs Antrobus asked.

"No," Georgie fairly shouted. It was now clear to whom 'he' applied.

"Oh, I thought Mr Griffiths was coming here today. That's what Piggy and Goosie said, anyway."

Rather than shout out an embarrassing denial, Georgie simply shook his head emphatically and made a vague motion in the general direction of the tea-urn, where Miss Mapp appeared to be deep in conversation with Colonel Boucher and the Quantocks.

Mrs Weston followed close behind, with Henry Luton pushing her bath-chair. She started talking almost as soon as she saw Georgie, with the result that she only came within earshot halfway through a sentence.

"...and so I said to Henry that we would be late, because I wanted to find my book of autographs for Mr Griffiths to sign, and I knew that I had last seen it in September – no, it must have been in October when I come to think about it because we'd had pheasant for dinner the night before, and you can only shoot pheasant in October, and this pheasant had been shot because there was some lead shot in it, which I always dislike. My aunt broke three teeth once on lead shot when she was eating a partridge, and from that day forward she never touched any game, not even a rabbit, and I can't say that I blame her, because it's never pleasant to go to the dentist. Mr Weston once had to go, and I told him that he shouldn't because the toothache would go away on its own, but he went anyway, and he had to have his head bound up for two weeks and we had to go to the chemist's three times for oil of cloves." She paused. "But where is Mr Griffiths?" she asked in bewilderment. "Perhaps he is with Daisy Quantock?"

"He is not here and I do not think Georgie Pillson expects him to be here," said Lucia in exasperation, answering for her host, who seemed to be engaged in dissuading Piggy and Goosie from gambolling over the croquet hoops. "Who has been spreading the story that he has attended this party, I wonder?"

"Why, it was Mr Georgie's sisters," Mrs Weston told her.

"But they are not in Riseholme. They have not been staying with Georgie, have they? Surely I would have heard if they had been here."

"No, my Elizabeth was shopping in Brinton for a nice piece of pork for my dinner because that new butcher on the High Street has some excellent cuts at a very reasonable price, and I'm sure I don't know how he does it with all the shortages that have been going on, but after all that's his business, I suppose. Anyway, Elizabeth told me that she was just coming out of the butchers, and she recognised them, riding bicycles down the street, in broad daylight, if you can imagine such a thing. So of course she said good morning to them – no, she told me it had just struck midday, so it would be afternoon – and they seemed to know who she was and asked if she lived in Riseholme and was her mistress Mrs Jane Weston, which is something she could hardly deny, now could she? So then they said that they had heard that Mr Pillson was having a garden party and that Mr Griffiths, the famous politician was invited. And so as I just said to you, I thought I couldn't let the occasion go by without obtaining his autograph, and so I am sorry I am late because I was looking for the book as I said to you just now."

"This is monstrous!" exclaimed Lucia. Pepino, who had been standing mutely observing these exchanges, quietly suggested that this might be a convenient time to meet Miss Mapp. He had of course heard all about Miss Mapp from Georgie, and had indeed observed her through his telescope (though since this instrument was of the astronomical persuasion, she had appeared as an Antipodean, that is to say with her heels in the air and head on the ground). Georgie therefore escorted the Lucases to Miss Mapp, where Pepino took Miss Mapp's extended hand, and muttered something about it being a pleasure to meet her.

"The pleasure is all mine, Mr Lucas. And Mr Pillson has been telling me all about how busy you all are. You must be exhausted, with not a moment to yourselves."

"Yes indeed," said Lucia. "But it is such a joy to be busy in such a manner, is it not, caro?"

"*Carissima*," he said in answer to Lucia's question. "I must beg to differ a little. Rather than 'busy', I would prefer to say that we are 'profitably and pleasurably enslaved in the service of Art'."

"What noble words!" exclaimed Miss Mapp. "Why, you are almost a poet, Mr Lucas!"

Pepino refrained from answering that he was indeed a poet, whose prose poems celebrated the glories of the human soul and its relationship with Nature and with Art, and whose works had been printed, albeit privately, and were available for the cognoscenti to read and enjoy.

Miss Mapp turned to Lucia. "Mr Pillson told me that you play the piano," Miss Mapp said.

"Might I possibly dare to ask you to play something for us later on? It would be such a treat."

Lucia, who had long since decided that her guests were to enjoy her rendering of the slow movement of Beethoven's 'Moonlight' sonata on Georgie's piano as the party drew to a close, allowed herself to be persuaded into agreeing to play later, as Foljambe arrived with a tray on which reposed several dishes of redcurrant fool.

Lucia could not help but notice the avidity with which Miss Mapp's hand reached for a dish, and the rapidity with which it emptied. Indeed, even while Foljambe and her tray were still within range of Miss Mapp's outstretched arm, she remarked how an empty dish was replaced on the tray, and another removed.

However entrancing the sight of Miss Mapp devouring several dishes of redcurrant fool might prove to be, it was Georgie with whom Lucia now wished to speak, regarding his sisters' reports of Mr Erddig Griffiths being present at his garden-party.

SEVENTEEN

She discovered Georgie in conversation with Colonel Boucher, but standing at some distance from him, on account of the bulldogs, which he found to be somewhat unnerving.

As soon as a suitable break appeared in the conversation, Lucia detached Georgie from the Colonel and his dogs, and fairly dragged him to a corner of the lawn where they would not be overheard.

"Georgie, when did you last see your sisters?" she enquired.

"Perhaps three months ago," he answered, after a few seconds' thought.

"You never told them that Mr Erddig Griffiths was coming to this garden-party?"

"Let me consider," he said thoughtfully. "They telephoned last week to say that they were making a cycling-tour and were passing through Brinton. They asked me if they could stay with me, but I told them that I was holding a garden-party on the day that they wanted to stay, and they said that they didn't want to attend. In fact, they were quite rude about the whole business. I think I made it up to them, though. I paid for their stay at the Crown in Brinton, since they weren't going to stay with me."

"Yes, yes," said Lucia impatiently. "But did you tell them about Mr Erddig Griffiths?"

"Why on earth are you asking me?" Georgie asked, clearly perplexed by this line of questioning.

"I'll tell you. You know that everybody has been coming here expecting to see this wretched Mr Griffiths now that he is famous, and I found out from Mrs Weston just now that her Elizabeth had met your sisters riding bicycles through Brinton and they had told her that this Griffiths person was coming here."

Georgie scratched his head (gently, to avoid dislodging his carefully arranged strands of hair). "How tarsome. I seem to remember now that I did mention him in the conversation I had with Hermy. I said that he was staying with the Quantocks."

"Then the mystery is solved," exclaimed Lucia. "It must be that they believed that he would still be in the village and that dear Daisy would not resist the temptation to show him off as her 'stunt' at this garden-party of yours."

Georgie shook his head. "I distinctly remember writing another letter to them after that to let them know that I had booked their room at the Crown, and I am sure that in the letter I mentioned that Mr Griffiths had left Riseholme. There is no reason at all for them to believe that Mr Griffiths is still staying with Daisy."

"That is, if they received your letter before they set off on their travels," Lucia pointed out.

"That is true," Georgie admitted.

"Then we must let it remain a mystery, though an annoying one, for now. We should return to your guests, especially Miss Mapp, who I am sure will feel neglected if no-one is talking to her."

Lucia need not have concerned herself about Elizabeth Mapp. It might be true that no-one was talking to her, but that is only because Miss Mapp herself was holding forth at voluble length on the glories of Tilling in general (with some subtle unfavourable comparisons to Riseholme), and of her Queen Anne house, Mallards, specifically. Her listeners, who appeared to be entranced by this stream of talk, had no opportunity to allow even a single word to make its way into the flow.

"Dear Miss Mapp," Lucia said to her, when a small gap appeared in the torrent of words into which Lucia could insert a sentence. "I believe there is a little more redcurrant fool, should you care to partake."

"Why, thank you so much," smiled Miss Mapp. "Most acceptable," she murmured, accepting a dish from the tray that Foljambe was holding ("Her fourth," said Mrs Antrobus in what was meant to be a whisper, but on account of her deafness ended up being clearly audible to those near her, and probably to Miss Mapp as well).

"Most acceptable," repeated Miss Mapp, as if she had not heard Mrs Antrobus's comment. "However, I believe my dear late grandmamma's recipe, though similar, might provide a welcome improvement. I shall send the recipe to Mr Pillson's cook."

There was an almost audible sucking of teeth from the assembled multitude. The redcurrant fool served at Georgie's garden-parties was, in the unquestioned opinion of all, quite simply the epitome of what redcurrant fool should be. In the collective opinion of Riseholme, it was impossible to improve on perfection. And Georgie, noble soul that he was, took no credit whatsoever for this, explaining that Foljambe had provided his cook with the recipe, and that all credit for this nectar of the gods was hers.

The result of Miss Mapp's pronouncement was a falling-off of her followers, both literal and metaphorical, so that in a very short space of time, she found herself holding an empty dish in one hand, and a spoon in the other, surrounded by an expanse of empty lawn.

Lucia, who had observed this little comedy with very mixed feelings, now entered the deserted scene, and presented herself once more in front of Miss Mapp.

"You were kind enough to invite me to play some music," she said. "No time like the present, is there?" Without waiting for an answer, she made her way into Georgie's house, drawing Miss Mapp after her on invisible strings.

Georgie, who had observed this, started to round up his guests, somewhat in the manner of a dog chasing errant sheep, and herding them, gently and politely, but in a manner that admitted of no dissent, into his parlour, where Lucia was already seated at the piano, moving her fingers in the air in a pattern that Georgie, and all who beheld her, instantly recognised as the opening triplets of Beethoven's 'Moonlight' sonata. Miss Mapp, for her part, was seated close by Lucia, an anticipatory smile on her face.

When all were still, and Piggy and Goosie had stopped their giggling, Lucia doled out the slow soulful triplets, in the manner of treacle dripping from a spoon. At the end, Miss Mapp, clearly unaware of the rites and customs of Tilling, lifted her head with a start (there were those who claimed that she also opened her eyes), and started to clap, stopping with an embarrassed look as she realised that no-one else was joining her. Then after a few seconds Pepino sighed, and the sigh was echoed by the whole room. Lucia, who had allowed her head to droop artistically as she played the final chord, lifted her eyes which, although apparently closed, had never missed a moment of what was going on (that is, if Georgie knew anything about the matter). She turned to Miss Mapp, who had turned an unbecoming shade of red. It was clearly incumbent on the visitor to say something.

"Dear Mrs Lucas, how much I enjoy those

quaint old tunes. So much we can learn from them is there not?" she gabbled.

Despite Lucia's admiration, amounting to almost worship, of Beethoven and his music, she would have been hard-pressed to provide a precise enumeration of anything that one could learn from the slow movement of the 'Moonlight'. She was as certain as she could be that Miss Mapp would find the task to be equally arduous, but rather than put this to the test, she invited Miss Mapp to take her place at the keyboard.

"Oh, no thank you, Mrs Lucas," was the answer. "I do have a sweet family instrument – a Blumenfeld, you know, which belonged to my Aunt Caroline. She was always considered to be a remarkably talented performer on the instrument."

"But you do play?" persisted Lucia.

"After such mastery of the keyboard as you have just displayed, I could not consider my efforts to be anything other than mere inept tinklings."

Lucia was reasonably certain that in this instance, Miss Mapp was stating nothing other than the truth, and decided to let the matter rest.

As was customary in Riseholme, the

performance of the Moonlight signified the end of a social event, and the guests began to depart. Miss Mapp took the hint, and started to leave for the Ambermere Arms.

Lucia, out of consideration for Foljambe and Georgie's cook, who had worked hard to provide an excellent afternoon's entertainment for the guests, had invited Georgie to supper at The Hurst.

"It will only be a little more than a tray," she had explained, "given how well you take care of your guests at your little get-togethers."

Georgie had accepted gladly. The kind of food that Lucia provided on such occasions was much to his taste. Even more to his taste was the slicing and dicing of the doings and sayings of the other Riseholmites over the course of the afternoon, and tonight there would be a special item on the menu in the form of Miss Elizabeth Mapp.

EIGHTEEN

As he had expected, Miss Mapp formed the major topic of conversation over the soup and Welsh rabbit that Lucia had provided.

"Four dishes!" exclaimed Lucia. "I wasn't counting, but Mrs Antrobus clearly had been doing so, and I'm afraid that she said it a bit too loudly for comfort. Hardly well-mannered, I thought," Lucia added. "If those are Tilling manners, then I, for one, am thankful not to be living there."

Pepino, who had been almost silent up to this point, spoke up. "I have to say that I considered it somewhat of a breach of good manners to make a comparison between her grandmother's recipe, and your excellent offering," he said.

"She did offer to send her grandmother's recipe," said Georgie, but his tone was more than a little dubious.

"We will see what we will see," said Lucia, darkly. "I have no doubt that it will turn out to be a cheap substitute for the real thing. A woman who will fight to the last halfpenny, I am sure."

Pepino expressed his puzzlement at this last.

"Her dress, caro," Lucia explained. "Make do and mend wasn't in it."

"I noticed that, too," said Georgie. He had a keen eye for details of dress, whether men's or women's. "I am certain that bodice has been through several sea-changes in its life." Usually Georgie would not have been so candid in his criticisms, but he had been more than a little put out by Miss Mapp's comments about the redcurrant fool.

"And I am almost certain," went on Lucia, "when she leaves the Ambermere Arms, that the landlord will face a list of complaints and demands that the bill he presents will be reduced. There seemed to be a certain – how shall I say it? – grabbiness, if I may be permitted to use the word, about her."

"And her embarrassment when she discovered that she was the only one applauding your performance of the Moonlight," said Georgie. "Poor thing." His tone of voice belied the words.

"Poor thing indeed," echoed Lucia. "She was no doubt somewhat embarrassed to find herself in company of a rather higher nature than she is used to in Tilling – her friend Major Flint, was it not, is of a lower rank than our own Colonel Boucher as the representative of His Majesty's Army? She clearly felt it necessary to bolster her high opinion of herself through her disparagement of our dear Riseholme and our little efforts to make the world a better place through Art and Culture."

"And that reminds me," said Pepino, rising from his seat, and moving to the sideboard. "I was going to give this to you this afternoon, carissima, but after seeing Miss Mapp, I decided that would be a little ostentatious." He presented Lucia with the small box that he had just removed from the sideboard.

"*Molto grazie*," Lucia said, opening the box. "Oh, a golden brooch. Very handsome indeed. Thank you so much." She paused and examined the jewellery a little closer. "But what is this in the middle? Hair?"

Pepino allowed himself a small smile. "I have

it on the best authority that it is indeed a lock of hair."

"But who would wish to wear such a thing?" said Lucia. Her initial enthusiasm seemed to have changed to something almost approaching disgust.

"Surely that would depend on whose hair it was?" suggested Georgie. He had previously been let into the secret of the provenance of the article – indeed, his opinion had been sought by Pepino regarding the suitability of the item as a gift, and he had wholeheartedly concurred that it was a most appropriate present for Lucia.

"I can think of few people whose hair I would wish to wear in a brooch," said Lucia. "Pepino, is this your hair?"

Her husband merely smiled and shook his head.

"Someone much older than Pepino," suggested Georgie. "Now sadly deceased, but his spirit lives on through music."

Light slowly dawned. "Not... Can this really be a lock of hair from the Master's head? From Beethoven himself?"

"I was assured that it is," said Pepino. "On my last trip to London I was passing a curio shop, and this was displayed in the window. So..." He let his words tail off.

Lucia was far from being demonstrative in her emotions, but it was clear to see that she was deeply moved by her husband's gift. Tears were visible in her sharp dark eyes, as she rose and kissed Pepino softly on the cheek. "Carissimo, you are too good to me."

"It is no more than you deserve," Pepino answered her.

EPILOGUE

Some weeks after this last, Georgie had invited the Lucases to dine with him. His cook had used the last of the asparagus to make a delicious soup, which was followed by a simple roast ham.

For the dessert, Georgie had prepared a little surprise. Foljambe brought in three dishes, an almost invisible smile on her face.

"Oh, your redcurrant fool, Foljambe!" exclaimed Lucia. "Thank you so much, Georgie for sharing what must be the last of your redcurrants with us."

However, after the first spoonful, Lucia's expression of anticipated pleasure turned sour.

"What is this, Georgie? Has your cook mislaid

the recipe? This is far below her usual standard, if I may say so."

Georgie exchanged glances with Foljambe, whose smile was now faintly visible.

"I must apologise," he said. "Miss Mapp of Tilling, whom you may remember—"

"I have done my best to expunge her from my memory, but yes, I do remember her," answered Lucia.

"She told me that she would send her grandmother's recipe for redcurrant fool. After she had read it, Cook told me that it looked as though it was rubbish. Even so, I asked her to use a portion of the redcurrants to make some of the recipe."

"She was right," said Pepino. "Maybe 'rubbish' is a rather harsh term, but it certainly is not up to the usual standard."

"Very well," said Georgie. "Foljambe, please clear away the Mapp fool, and bring in the dessert that Cook has created using your recipe – the proper one."

"With pleasure, sir," replied Foljambe, and the smile was now clearly visible on her face as she removed the offending dishes and spoons.

When the replacement had been served and enjoyed by all, Lucia spoke up. "Thank you for an excellent meal, Georgie. I am sure that there is no house in Tilling that could match the food we have just eaten."

"Nor the company in which it was eaten," offered Georgie gallantly. He raised his glass. "I would like to offer a toast." The others grasped the stem of their glass. "To Riseholme."

"To Riseholme," the others echoed, as their glasses clinked together.

IF YOU ENJOYED THIS STORY...

$\mathbf{P}$lease consider writing a review on a Web
site such as Amazon or Goodreads.

You may also enjoy some adventures of
Sherlock Holmes by Hugh Ashton, who has
been described in *The District Messenger*, the
newsletter of the Sherlock Holmes Society of
London, as being "one of the best writers of
new Sherlock Holmes stories, in both plotting
and style".

Volumes published so far include :

Tales from the Deed Box of John H. Watson M.D.

More from the Deed Box of John H. Watson M.D.

Secrets from the Deed Box of John H. Watson M.D.

The Darlington Substitution (novel)

Notes from the Dispatch-Box of John H. Watson M.D.

*Further Notes from the Dispatch-
box of John H. Watson M.D.*

The Death of Cardinal Tosca (novel)

*The Last Notes from the Dispatch-
box of John H. Watson, M.D.*

The Trepoff Murder (ebook only)

1894

Without my Boswell

Some Singular Cases of Mr. Sherlock Holmes
The Lichfield Murder
The Adventure of the Bloody Steps
The Adventure of Vanaprastha (ebook only)

Children's detective stories, with beautiful illustrations by Andy Boerger, the first of which was nominated for the prestigious Caldecott Prize :

Sherlock Ferret and the Missing Necklace
Sherlock Ferret and The Multiplying Masterpieces
Sherlock Ferret and The Poisoned Pond
Sherlock Ferret and the Phantom Photographer
The Adventures of Sherlock Ferret

Short stories, thrillers, alternative history, and historical science fiction titles:

Tales of Old Japanese
At the Sharpe End
Balance of Powers
Beneath Gray Skies
Red Wheels Turning
Angels Unawares
The Untime
The Untime Revisited
Unknown Quantities
Mapp at Fifty
Mapp's Return

Full details of all of these and more at :
https://HughAshtonBooks.com

ABOUT THE AUTHOR

Hugh Ashton was born in the United Kingdom, and moved to Japan in 1988, where he lived until his return to the UK in 2016.

He is best known for his Sherlock Holmes stories, which have been hailed as some of the most authentic pastiches on the market, and have received favourable reviews from Sherlockians and non-Sherlockians alike.

He has also published other work in a number of genres, including alternative history, historical science fiction, and thrillers, based in Japan, the USA, and the UK.

He currently lives in the historic city of Lichfield with his wife, Yoshiko.

His ramblings may be found on Facebook, Twitter, and in various other places on the Internet. He may be contacted at: author@HughAshtonBooks.com